HER MERCENARY

AMANDA MCKINNEY

AMANDA MCKINNEY

Paperback ISBN 978-1-7358681-9-6
eBook ISBN 978-1-7358681-8-9

Editor(s):
Nancy Brown, Redline Proofreading
Pam Berehulke, Bulletproof Editing
Cover Design:
Damonza

https://www.amandamckinneyauthor.com

DEDICATION

For Mama

ALSO BY AMANDA

Amanda McKinney writing as AMANDA TISEVICH:

The Stone Secret - A Thriller Novel

A Marriage of Lies- A Thriller Novel

Thriller Novella Series:

The Widow of Weeping Pines

The Raven's Wife

The Lie Between Us

The Keeper's Closet

Latest Romantic Suspense Series - ON THE EDGE:

Buried Deception

Trail of Deception

BESTSELLING STEELE SHADOWS SERIES:

Cabin 1 (Steele Shadows Security)

Cabin 2 (Steele Shadows Security)

Cabin 3 (Steele Shadows Security)

Phoenix (Steele Shadows Rising)

Jagger (Steele Shadows Investigations)

Ryder (Steele Shadows Investigations)

Her Mercenary (Steele Shadows Mercenaries)

Her Renegade (Steele Shadows Mercenaries) - Coming 2024

AWARDS AND RECOGNITION

JAGGER (STEELE SHADOWS INVESTIGATIONS)
*2021 Daphne du Maurier Award for Excellence in
Mystery/Suspense 2nd Place Winner*

RATTLESNAKE ROAD
*Named one of POPSUGAR's 12 Best Romance Books to Have a
Spring Fling With
2022 Silver Falchion Finalist*

REDEMPTION ROAD
2022 Silver Falchion Finalist

THE STORM
*Winner of the 2018 Golden Leaf for Romantic Suspense
2018 Maggie Award for Excellence Finalist
2018 Silver Falchion Finalist
2018 Beverley Finalist
2018 Passionate Plume Honorable Mention Recipient*

THE FOG

Winner of the 2019 Golden Quill for Romantic Suspense
Winner of the 2019 I Heart Indie Award for Romantic Suspense
2019 Maggie Award of Excellence Finalist
2019 Stiletto Award Finalist

CABIN 1 (STEELE SHADOWS SECURITY)

2020 National Readers Choice Award Finalist
2020 HOLT Medallion Finalist

THE CAVE

2020 Book Buyers Best Finalist
2020 Carla Crown Jewel Finalist

DIRTY BLONDE

2017 2nd Place Winner for It's a Mystery Contest

LET'S CONNECT!

Text **AMANDABOOKS to 66866** to sign up
for Amanda's Newsletter and get the latest
on new releases, promos, and freebies!
Or, you can sign up below.

https://www.amandamckinneyauthor.com

HER MERCENARY

She was supposed to be the mission. She became his undoing.

When American schoolteacher Samantha Greene goes missing in Mexico, the US government calls on private military firm, Astor Stone Inc., to assist in finding her. Former soldier Roman Thieves volunteers for the case, seizing the opportunity to kill two birds with one stone. After-all, no one knows the dark underworld of human trafficking like he does—or knows exactly how involved he is in their business dealings.

When the mission falls apart, Roman finds himself on the run with the blonde-haired, green-eyed bombshell, seeking refuge in the untamed wilderness of the Sierra Madre Mountains—on a trail rumored to be haunted, nonetheless. With only a small bag of provisions, they must battle the elements, including scorching hot temperatures, and work together to outsmart the savage predators hunting them.

As his motives become clouded by a fierce need to protect Sam, Roman must choose between avenging his past and saving the woman who snuck her way into his heart.

ASTOR STONE, INC.

- CLASSIFIED -

Contract for Services of Astor
Stone, Inc.

PARTIES TO THE AGREEMENT:

This Contract For Services is made
effective as of September 12, 2001
(the Effective Date), by and between
the Parties: Astor Stone, of Astor
Stone, Inc. (Astor Stone, Inc.); and
the Government of the United States of
America (the US Government).

DESCRIPTION OF SERVICES:

Astor Stone, Inc. hereby agrees to
provide the US Government with clan-

destine operations, including, but not
limited to, the planning and execution
of highly classified extraction,
assassination, and intelligence-gath-
ering missions, both within and
outside of US borders, under the terms
and conditions hereby agreed upon by
the Parties as defined in Appendix A.
Astor Stone, Inc. shall receive orders
directly from the United States
Central Intelligence Agency and/or the
United States Department of Defense,
and is to operate independently from
the US Government, concealing US
Government involvement in said orders.
The US Government is not responsible
for injuries or casualties and will
deny all knowledge of Astor Stone,
Inc. and its agents.

TERM:

Contract renews on a yearly basis
pending formal review of completed
missions. The contract may be extended
and/or renewed by agreement of all
Parties in writing thereafter.

PAYMENT:

The US Government agrees to pay Astor
Stone, Inc. $1,500,000 USD per
mission, distributed as follows:

$750,000 paid on receipt of orders, and $750,000 paid upon mission completion. Bonuses may be paid on a mission-based basis, as determined by the US Government.

1

ROMAN

Dublin, Ireland – Thirty years ago

I ducked behind a dumpster, careful to avoid the beam of moonlight cutting through the alley.

Ahead was a vacant city block, littered with discarded trash, paper cups, wrappers, and needles. A plastic bag, caught in the icy wind, tumbled across the cracked concrete before snagging in a barbwire fence.

Beyond the barrier, a line of homeless people shuffled anxiously from foot to foot, bundled in scarves, some in trash bags, a few wrapped in silver solar blankets provided to them by the Catholic church down the street. Most were women and children, waiting to receive their scraps from the food bank around the corner.

All heads turned to the two men crossing the street, the men I'd been following for seven blocks.

The homeless eyed the men warily. They were obvious strangers to this part of town in their black suits, cashmere coats, and fancy dress shoes.

I knew, however, that these men were no strangers to this neighborhood. They'd been here many times before, under the cover of night.

I use the term "men" loosely, as one of the suits couldn't have been much older than myself. I guessed maybe seventeen or eighteen, although I'd never seen his face. With the swagger in his stride, he seemed older, wearing an air of confidence much like his companion, a much older and taller man.

A twinge of envy gripped me. Not just in the way the men dressed and the fact that they obviously had money, but in the way they carried themselves with such confidence and self-assurance, such strength. Such intent in their stride.

Despite being in one of the poorest neighborhoods in Dublin, these men strode through the streets like they owned them. I admired that. I admired the way they made people cross to the other side of the street when they approached. The seas parted for these men.

I wondered what it would be like to be as respected, as feared as they were.

I wanted that. I wanted people to look at me the way they did these two men.

It was the fourth time I'd seen them in over a month. Each time, they'd pass by the diner on the corner, lingering by the windows before disappearing in the shadows.

And with each time, my instinct grew stronger. These men were associated with the bastards who owned my mother. I was sure of it.

Careful to stay down, I darted across the alley, skirting the dilapidated brick apartment buildings littered with graffiti. Gripping closed the thin jacket I'd stolen from the gas station with one hand, I checked for the small kitchen knife

I always carried in my pocket. A habit I'd developed over the years.

A side door opened. A man and woman stumbled out, the pungent scent of ammonia and chemicals following a moment later. *Meth.* I froze in place, watching as they jerked their way to the street, the man incessantly dragging his fingernails down his neck.

Mindlessly, my hand went to my arm, scratching the rash of tiny blisters on my own wrists.

When the tweakers rounded the corner and disappeared, I refocused on the men in suits. They paused under the overhang of an abandoned building, appearing to be waiting for something.

I slipped into the shadows, watching them from behind as they studied the diner.

Seconds turned into minutes.

An icy blast of wind swept through the alleyway, carrying with it the scent of spoiled bacon and cabbage. My stomach growled.

The men began walking again, heading straight for the diner.

Quickly, silently, I jogged down the sidewalk, hugging the buildings while navigating through the shadows. My pulse rate increased, my instincts sensing something in the air.

This time, instead of lingering outside the diner windows, the suits strode past, disappearing around the block.

Frowning, I paused, slipping into a doorway and out of sight. Something was different. Something was off.

I studied the diner. Just beyond the barred windows, silhouettes moved inside the small restaurant, none of which belonged to my short, lean mother.

I scanned the block, spotting her red truck parked along the curb. She was definitely still at work. My heart started to pound.

Passing by the diner window wasn't an option, because if my mother saw me, as she undoubtedly would, she would scold me for being out past dark. I would cause her worry, and probably earn a slap on the wrist for me making her leave her shift to drag me home by the ear.

Where the hell had the men gone?

Another minute passed as I surveyed the block, cataloging everything around me. The rusty cars, the old shopping carts, the line of the starving homeless.

"Fuck it." I stepped out of the shadows, flipped up my collar, shoved my hands in my pockets, and strode down the sidewalk, retracing the steps of the men. The wind was biting, stinging my cheeks and blurring my vision as I quickly passed the diner and rounded the block.

I stopped and looked around.

No one.

Feeling again for the knife in my pocket, I continued forward until reaching the alley behind the diner where my mother worked. Steam rolled from the street vents, obscuring the alleyway.

My stomach vibrated with nerves as I pulled the knife from my pocket and stepped through the steam. There they were, two looming silhouettes, the sharp outline of their suits punctuating the gravity of the moment.

The older one turned, and I stopped.

We stared at each other, faceless men in the dirty alley. The outline of a knife twinkled from the man's hand. The shorter one, whose face I never saw, turned and hurried in the opposite direction.

My instinct that something was wrong skyrocketed.

Gripping the splintered hilt of my knife, I advanced on the large silhouette. Though I couldn't see his face, nor he mine, I knew without question his eyes were locked on me.

Until I saw the dying ember of a cigarette butt at his feet, the smoke swirling upward, catching on the wind. The pale, delicate hand lying limp next to it.

I lunged forward, focusing on the body lying in a crumpled heap on the cold concrete. My heart seizing, I recognized the curly auburn hair, the small stature, the tattered blue coat.

"Mom!" I screamed, dropping to my knees, no longer caring about the man in the suit. Tears welled in my eyes as I gently rolled her over.

Her head lolled to the side, strands of auburn tickling across a pair of glassy green eyes, staring blankly up at the night sky. A circle of deep crimson colored her stomach, and a growing bloodstain spread over her blue coat.

I opened my mouth to talk to her, to say something, anything, but nothing came out. Carefully, I pulled open the flaps of the coat. My mother had been stabbed repeatedly in the abdomen.

My mother had been murdered.

My tears freezing, I stilled, the realization igniting a fire that swept through me in a hysterical rage that I quite literally felt consuming my body.

I dropped my mother from my arms, her dead body landing with a thud on the concrete. Slowly, I rose, no longer human. Instead, I was an animal, feral, wild with fury, tunnel-visioned on my prey.

I left my mother's body lying there in the middle of the alley while I chased down the man who killed her. She lay, dead in her own blood, as I tackled the man in the suit and shoved my knife into his throat.

For the rest of my life, I'll never forget his face. His stoic expression as the tip of the knife opened his skin. The way his gaze pierced mine as I dragged the blade across his jugular. His expression wasn't one of fear or panic. Instead, the man stared at me with an intensity that turned my blood to ice.

Never once did his eyes leave mine.

Never once, as I watched the first man I'd killed take his last breath. The first of many to come.

In that single moment, that night in the slums of Dublin, I rewrote my path, my life, my goals, what I would become. It solidified the monster I would become.

Just like him.

I still see those eyes every night when I close mine. Taunting me, guiding me, hypnotically keeping my head underwater as I navigate revenge.

There's no way out. The man in the suit now owns me.

There's no way out.

Not until I find the other man. The one who got away.

2

SAM

The present

It was an invisible yet undeniable presence, a thick, sticky mass that spread to the corners of the room, consuming everything in its path.

Heavy and wet, the hot, humid air coated my skin like a layer of Vaseline. It was stifling in that small room, like sucking air through a straw, getting just enough oxygen to stay alive but never enough to thrive.

This is what I will always remember of that time. The humidity. The dank heat in that concrete basement. So severe, it was like a third person trapped in there with me, an omnipresent tormentor with no concept of day or night.

The nostalgia triggered from the smell of ocean air has been rewritten in my brain. The sour, briny scent once associated with Mai Tais and sunblock will now forever remind me of a pit where discarded humans were thoughtlessly tossed and held against their will.

There was a time that I didn't believe in hell. An eternal

optimist, maybe, but I believed that the chosen were lifted to the heavens, while the "others" decomposed, returning to the earth, their souls simply fading into thin air like smoke from a cigarette catching on the wind.

The chosen would receive the gift of peace, living— whatever that looked like—in true contentment, while the bodies of the others would remain on earth, only to be forgotten, nameless faces slowly slipping from the binds of the flesh. They would become nothing, the ultimate punishment.

Now, though, I have a very different perspective on heaven and hell, good and evil, for I have seen real-life demons up close and personal.

Hell is not the afterlife. It is the now.

It is very present, in the dark corners of the world where the most vile, savage sins are committed. Where humans are nothing more than animals, devoid of morals and decency, and instead driven by carnal needs like lust and greed. There is no restraint, no respect, no dignity, only shameless surrender to sexual needs and urges. Human, animal, beast, or child, no one is safe on this path.

It is very real, this morally bankrupt, corrupt playground that I will forever consider hell on earth.

"That would never happen to me."

How many times have you said those words? Thought them?

I certainly had. I was one of those people, the naive small-town girl who thought, *Nope, that kind of stuff doesn't happen around here.*

How foolish I was.

Now I sing a very different tune, because the girl who grew up playing softball and wearing second-hand Converses, the girl whose biggest worry was whether she would get a date for the prom, became a statistic at age twenty-nine. I became a name, a headshot in one of those horrific news stories that steals your attention for only a minute before you turn away, pushing it away, and think, *That would never happen to me.*

I was a normal, nothing-special woman with no criminal record, no dark past, no addictions—aside from coffee, though who considers that an addiction anymore? I was just normal. Like someone you know. Like you, perhaps. I didn't hang out with the wrong crowd; I didn't tempt fate. I just trudged through life doing the best I could with what I had.

Divorced, single, discontent.

Nothing—*nothing*—in my life suggested that I, this average woman, would find myself abducted and thrown into hell on earth . . . most of me yet to return.

The woman who was taken that fateful night wasn't the same woman in this cage. I lost a piece of my soul during my captivity, that childlike joyful spirit that delights in the small things. I lost my roots, my core.

Essentially, I lost myself.

One day, maybe I'll be able to reflect on what happened without having a physical reaction. One day, maybe I'll slip into those Converses again and try to remember what it was like to be normal. Who I once was.

3

ROMAN

*H*er name was Samantha Greene, age twenty-nine, divorced, seventh-grade schoolteacher from Fairhope, Oklahoma, population five thousand. Five-foot-four, blond hair, hazel eyes, and a weight of 120 pounds, this according to her driver's license.

Additional details not included: the slight bump in the middle of her nose that freckles in the summer. The faded scar above her right eyebrow, the one that she furrows when deep in concentration. The coral flecks in her irises—a color I'd never seen before—shimmer almost eerily like a cat's when the light catches them just so. The ridiculously long, feathered lashes that emphasize this aforementioned feline resemblance. And then there's the round, feminine mouth that appears to be stuck in a perpetual pout.

Her lips stole my focus for longer than I care to admit, but her eyes are what got me. I'm unsure why. They were the kind of eyes that seemed to peer directly into your soul. Tried to figure you out. In every photograph, every social media post, every article I'd dug up, Samantha Greene (known as Sam) was always smiling.

Fairhope happened to have a Peeping Tom that summer. The sick fuck would reposition CCTV cameras to peer into unsuspecting women's apartments and homes. I discovered that Samantha Greene was one of his victims.

I'd hacked into the CCTV feed from the camera across the street from her apartment, which pointed directly into her living room window. The street cam had been strategically positioned by the Peeping Tom, a lecherous, metrosexual twenty-something named Blade Barney. Barney, and his unfortunate last name—only slightly worse than the first—was a Fairhope police department new-hire, addicted to both fake tanning and BDSM pornography, the latter revealed to the chief of police by an anonymous tip.

Blade Barney no longer works for the FPD.

While the camera has since been repositioned, the images were forever burned into my brain.

I knew the most intimate details about Samantha Greene. I'd memorized every line of her face, every curve of her body. Her entire internet footprint. I'd interviewed her friends, family, coworkers.

She was my mission.

I knew that Samantha began her day with a cup of coffee. No creamer, no sugar—black and strong. Supercharged, according to the label on the boxes that arrived at her door monthly, ordered from a specialty shop online. *Store-bought coffee isn't good enough for this junior high teacher* was my first note about the woman.

Every morning, with her dog at her feet, Miss Greene watches the local news while sipping the ridiculously overpriced coffee beans. I don't know why this bothers me so much. Perhaps because her car is badly in need of new tires, or because her reading glasses are held together with Scotch tape.

Anyway. This morning ritual is spent wrapped in the same blanket every morning, on the same dated leather couch, in a nightshirt that reads I CANNOT TEACH ANYBODY ANYTHING, I CAN ONLY MAKE THEM THINK – SOCRATES.

Sidenote: I've decided that Miss Greene must have a dozen replicas of this nightshirt as I refuse to believe that a woman would wear the same nightshirt multiple nights in a row.

Like clockwork, Samantha arrives at Fairhope Middle School at exactly 7:25 every morning. Here, she dedicates her life to preparing the youth of society to become mature, productive adults.

Ten hours later, Samantha gets into her banged-up Subaru (which is one pothole away from falling apart like a bad game of Jenga) and drives home—unless it's Wednesday. On Wednesdays she goes to the grocery store, the liquor store, then home.

There, she spends the evening grading papers, developing lesson plans and instructional materials for the days and weeks to come. On the rare event that Miss Greene drinks three beers instead of her usual two, she browses a dating website while humming to her favorite 2000s dance-hits playlist on the radio. She prefers Bud Lite to Miller Lite, although I've decided not to hold this against her.

According to public record, Samantha has been divorced eight years, after a fleeting marriage to her high school boyfriend. It appears that she has no man—or woman, for that matter—in her life, despite the dating site she frequents where I discovered, somewhat unexpectedly, that her username is @Mrs_Frizzle_Dizzle.

After much research, I realized this username is a nod to the adventurous and fun-loving teacher from the old cartoon, *The Magic School Bus.* I also realized that Miss Greene has an odd sense of humor.

A few evenings a month, from six to seven, Miss Greene offers free tutoring at the local library to her students. (I think they call her "Dizzle" here. Weirder than that, I think she likes it.)

It's obvious that these students are the number one priority in her life. Her dog, whose appearance could give Nick Nolte's mug shot a run for its money, is a close second. And in a distant third place, the overpriced coffee beans . . . and an unnatural aversion to laundry that makes me itch.

This is the extent of Samantha Greene's life. It's Groundhog Day, over and over again.

Otherwise known as my hell.

Of the five personality traits, Samantha Greene sits solidly in the Agreeableness (warm, cooperative, needs to be liked) and Conscientiousness (practical, organized, devoted) groupings.

According to this, I can conclude that Miss Greene is a cautious optimist who defines her life by dedication to a cause—in this case, teaching. In the event that this cause is ripped away from her, her identity will come into question. In other words, when I find her, I can expect an extremely emotional and mentally fragile train wreck, assuming she's still alive.

In summary, this woman is my polar opposite. This is irrelevant, and I'm unsure why I've contemplated these differences so much.

Perhaps it's the age difference. She's just a kid, while I'm slowly being sucked into middle age. Two days after Samantha turned twenty-nine, I turned forty-two, though I feel much older. Most days, my brain is at war with my body. But because I consider fatigue a weakness, I push myself until I end up with a pulled muscle or face-first on the floor, whichever comes first. I'm not as fast as I once was. Some days I don't feel as strong.

I can't remember the last time I laughed.

While Samantha is the type of person who assumes that humans will always do the right thing when provided the opportunity, I believe that people will do only what suits them when given the opportunity. Trust is something I lost long ago, while Samantha has built a career around making others feel comfortable around her and trust her.

People don't feel comfortable around me. It's just as well, as I find being in public spaces as painful as listening to pop-hit radio—especially the 2000s.

Last night, I lay in bed wondering what Miss Greene would think of me. What she would think if she knew how many men I've killed. How many people I've deceived. How many identities I've had. How many secrets I have.

And why is this turning into an assessment about me?

You might be wondering if, at this point, I'm a stalker—or worse, for that matter.

I'm not. (Though "worse" is subjective.)

It's my job to know every detail, every tic, every fear, every passion of my target. The moment I accept a mission, I begin compiling a detailed file on the target. I learned long ago that this information is vital for a smooth extraction. Knowing—and being ready to adapt to—how the target might react to any given situation can literally make or break a mission.

And there is no mission more important to me than the one I am about to embark on.

On August third, Samantha Greene traveled to Puerto Vallarta, Mexico, for a bachelorette party with five of her childhood friends.

Only five of those six women returned.

The American schoolteacher was last seen leaving a bar downtown alone, texting on her cell phone. She never made it back to her hotel.

This is where I come in. My mission is to find, extract, and deliver Samantha Greene back to the States.

Dead or alive.

4

SAM

a fly landed on the tip of my nose.

I focused on the sensation of its tiny legs, the small, fleshy spongelike mouth tapping its way over my sweat-slicked skin, sucking up the secretions of my pores. It soon tired of me and zipped away, resettling on the bucket that held my feces.

There was one sickly oscillating fan in the corner of the room. Someone had positioned it eight feet under a small hopper window that had been installed inches from the concrete ceiling. The dusty blades failed miserably to cool the space, instead succeeding only in stirring the foul odor of the room.

Day in and day out, I focused on the whirring white noise, forcing myself into some sort of meditative state in an attempt to calm the crippling anxiety. I knew every whine of that fan, the sharp squeal when it turned to the left, and the three successive taps when it slowly stuttered back to the right.

The cacophonous ballad became a weird kind of

centering for me. To this day, I wonder if without it, I would have completely gone mad.

I'd been given a thin blue housedress, the kind you would find on the discount racks at Walmart. It had holes and was four sizes too large. No shoes or socks. No bra.

No panties.

I'd been in captivity fourteen days at that point. I know this because with each sunrise, I'd scratch a mark into my forearm. In that time, I'd watched over a dozen others forced in and out of those basement doors, each in worse shape than the last.

Yet, I'd remained. I was the only woman in the basement who hadn't been moved, sold, or replaced. I was the only woman who hadn't been beaten or raped.

And I had absolutely no idea why.

Turning, I surveyed the brunette teen who had been dragged in hours earlier, now curled into a ball next to the bucket in her cage. I guessed her age to be fifteen or sixteen. She was lying in the sunlight pooling in from the hopper window, the only beam of light in the entire room. Under a spotlight, I mused, chained at the ankle just as I was.

Her cage was directly across from mine, the third one down in a line of steel storage lockers that were barely tall enough to stand in and about four feet wide.

There were other victims in the cages in the room, but I never saw their faces. These victims remained still and silent. Sometimes in the night, I could hear them stir. I imagined them as creatures more than humans, pale gray zombies, crawling on all fours. I know now that they had been continually drugged by the guards, slowly becoming addicted to heroin in an attempt to make them more reliant and submissive to the captors.

I still have nightmares about them.

The brunette was curled into the fetal position, weeping, her jerking shudders shaking her body. Occasionally, she would scream out, a long, hair-raising howl that for a moment—just a moment—would drown out the deafening beat of the mariachi music upstairs.

I watched her closely, wondering what her story was.

Her long dark brown hair spiraled in beautiful locks down her back, hair most women would kill for. She was wearing a yellow sundress, a bit short, one that a rebellious teen might wear to brunch with her family on vacation while trying to catch the eye of the handsome young waiter.

Had she wandered too far from the resort? Met a man and was persuaded into free drinks behind the bar? Or had she been stumbling back to her hotel, mindlessly texting her friends, when she was snatched off the street seconds before a needle pierced her neck.

We'd yet to speak to each other.

I wasn't even sure if she knew I was there. Or if she spoke English, for that matter.

I considered saying something, attempting to console her, but what to say?

I knew her story would be similar to mine. I knew that, eventually, her tears would dry. The fear and sadness would be replaced with the grit of survival—or would it?

Would there come a point in her captivity where she would stop crying and begin searching for something in her cage to kill herself with? Anything to stop the pain, the fear, the life no longer worth living?

In the first few days of my captivity, I fought my circumstances. I was determined to escape, to not give in to them. I spent every second of every day trying to figure out how to do this. I promised myself that I wouldn't lose who I was. That I wouldn't lose the strength my mother had instilled in me. Told myself that these motherfuckers would regret the day they took me.

Until the day they forced me to watch a woman being gang-raped. In the two weeks of my captivity, this was the only time I'd considered suicide.

But then, something deep inside me surged to life. A desire to survive. This is what kept me alive during those days.

A sudden bang startled me, pulling my attention to the rickety wood door.

The brunette shot up to a seated position. She glanced at me, her red-rimmed eyes wild with fear.

I steeled my spine and stared back, sending her a subliminal message of strength.

Don't let them see you cry, I internally begged her, knowing that the bastards got off on this.

Don't let them see you cry.

Don't let them see you cry.

The click of the locks turning and unlocking echoed like gunshots in the room. One after the other, the *click, click, click* ratcheting up the tension like the slow, haunting music in a scary movie right before the slaying.

Despite my subliminal message not to scream, the brunette did just that. She scrambled backward, pressing herself against the back of the cage. I felt a sudden urge to slap her—to slap sense into her like a mother might her troublemaking teenager.

The door opened and a harsh, violent beam of light sliced through the dark room. In the beginning, I would turn away and close my eyes from the light. Now I stared into it, a part of me wishing the light would steal my vision. Blind me from the horrors around me.

The man they called Capitán descended the small staircase. As usual, his pace was slow and threatening as he scanned his slaves with his one good eye. The other was covered by a black eye patch, which somehow made him even more terrifying. Despite an unimpressive daily uniform of faded army fatigues and scuffed black combat boots, Capitán carried an air of arrogance and authority that the other men didn't own.

I looked down. I'm ashamed to admit this.

Eye contact with the guards was forbidden.

My heart pounded in time with each step of Capitán's boots. I didn't know his real name. Although I spoke little to no Spanish, I tried to pick up what I could in the conversations around me. But I never got his name.

Two guards followed him into the basement, neither of whom I recognized.

Over the course of my captivity, I gathered that something big was happening soon. That we were going to be taken somewhere, for something. And the time was ticking down, the movement around me becoming more frequent and frantic.

Capitán approached my cage first.

I kept my gaze down but held my shoulders back, a ridiculous thing I did to appear strong and unafraid. Unaffected by him. Or perhaps to convince myself of this.

I waited, focusing on the sound of the fan. The whirl, the *tap*, the whirl, *tap, tap, tap.*

With a dismissive sniff, Capitán turned away from me and approached the brunette, who was now whimpering like an abused puppy. The guards followed in his wake.

The lock was released and the cage door creaked open. The girl was dragged out. Her scream raised every single hair on my arms as the guards subdued her.

Finally, silence.

I closed my eyes as she was carried upstairs, as if that somehow erased what was happening around me.

For the hundredth time, I asked myself, *Why not me?* Why had I not been mercilessly beaten or raped? Why was I being spared?

What did they have planned for me? The knowing that I was somehow different from the others, the anticipation of figuring out why and eventually what was to come, was worse than being raped.

I'd convinced myself that I was a sacrifice of sorts. Soon to be nailed to a cross and gutted like a pig in some satanic ritual.

Little did I know at the time, I was nothing more than bait. A pawn in a dangerous game between two ruthless, savage men.

5

ROMAN

Mexico City, Mexico

$\mathcal{I}$ glanced at my watch as I stepped off the elevator and into an air-conditioned wall of air scented with tropical perfume and pheromones. It was 12:17 a.m.

I was early. I'm always early.

Laughter mingled with the five-piece mariachi band playing softly in the shadows. Candlelight danced off mirrored walls and floor-to-ceiling windows that overlooked the *real* city that never sleeps.

Executives and politicians networked in suits and ties, posturing for the whores who patiently mingled around them, waiting for the perfect time to strike. Always after midnight, they moved in for the kill, when the line between fact and fiction became blurred and decisions became poor. When import beer was replaced with top-shelf liquor, and wedding rings were slipped into pockets.

And then there were the businessmen. Some were legitimate economic leaders. Most were not, however, and were drinking on behalf of high-ranking drug lords or cartel leadership, hoping to cut deals with aforementioned executives and politicians.

Whether friend or foe, all were packing heat.

Sugar Skull was the type of high-end establishment that required prior approval of entry, where bottles of three-thousand-dollar champagne were served with appetizers, gunshots were silenced, and bodies magically disappeared without a trace before the dessert was even served.

It was my playground, operating exactly as I'd intended when I bought the place five years earlier.

"Oh!" A bleached-blond hostess stepped in front of me with the eagerness of a goldendoodle, and probably an IQ to match. "Mr. Thieves, hi. Lovely to see you again."

The young woman's black dress was four inches too short, and her breasts five sizes too large for the bones she considered a healthy body. She was new to the establishment, and I made a mental note to take this up with the manager. I was to know every employee who came through the front doors. Although she knew who I was, having obviously been briefed on who I was ahead of time, I'd never seen her before.

I stepped around her, the foul mood I'd awoken with now simmering with annoyance.

"W—wait." The tick of high heels pounded the marble floor behind me. "Mr. Thieves, may I escort you to your—"

"No. Thank you."

Ignoring the glances from patrons, I wove my way through the dim, crowded room, deftly plucking a bottle of Pappy Van Winkle off a table of drunk politicians. Based on the men's preoccupation with a foursome of women half their age, they'd never miss it, though the women might.

The bar was packed, bodies everywhere, loud chatter,

drunken laughter, pops of light against shadows. Noise, noise, *noise.*

Loosening the tie around my neck, I slid into the back corner booth, flicking a pile of discarded napkins onto the floor. Facing the door, I pressed my back against the wall, resting my hand on the pistol under my suit jacket.

"Mr. Thieves, may I offer you an iced glass with that bottle you just swiped from the senator's table?"

"Please." I turned my gaze to the waitress advancing on the table. "And a plate of habanero chicken wings, with ranch—extra ranch."

"I don't need to tell you that the kitchen is closed—"

"Just like you don't need to tell me you'll have them out for me in under ten minutes."

The waitress grinned, a pair of sharp bright blue eyes twinkling against a weathered face and long gray hair. Though *waitress* was her formal title, Francisca served as my eyes and ears in the bar while I wasn't there.

Francisca Lopez, a sixty-four-year-old former corrections officer, had waitressed at Sugar Skull since the day I watched her body-slam a pickpocket outside of La Merced Market. She'd manhandled the kid—who was twice her weight—pinning him in place until the authorities arrived. I offered her a job right there on the bloody sidewalk.

At six-foot-one, Francisca was an intimidating presence, despite the long, traditional *huipiles* she wore every day. The tunic-like dresses were an effort to be feminine, I guessed. But what do I know about that?

She bent down, collecting the napkins I'd flicked away earlier and tossing them into a nearby trash can. "The chef prepared caviar and crème fraîche tartlets for your arrival this evening."

"I'd rather have my balls slammed in a car door, Francisca."

"I don't need to hear about your extracurricular activities, Mr. Thieves." She winked. "I'll get those hillbilly chicken wings out immediately." She set a fresh napkin on the table, and the sweating glass on top.

"Is that a new perfume?" I asked.

"Why yes, it is." She cocked one gray brow. "And what do you want to know about it?"

"I want to know who got it for you."

"So you can run him off like you did the last one?"

"You deserve better than a deadbeat father with two DWIs under his belt, Ms. Lopez."

"I know."

And she did. The woman was as confident and sure of herself as any I'd met before her. Problem was, Francisca was eternally lonely. Understandable, I guess, after losing her only two sons to gang-related gunfights, then dedicating her life to law enforcement to help ensure no other mother would experience the torment she had.

A torment I knew far too well.

Francisca blew out a breath. "Truth?"

"There's no other option between us."

"I bought the perfume myself." She smiled softly, almost sheepishly. "Turns out, my rent has been paid for the entire year by an anonymous Irish businessman with more wealth than he knows what to do with." Emotion sparkled in her eyes.

I dipped my chin.

Francisca sniffed, then looked away, shaking off the pesky emotions. I didn't do sentimental thank-yous, and she knew that.

"Anyway," she said with a smile, "because of this little surprise, I bought myself a bottle of nice perfume."

"Good for you. Now, tell me why you bought it."

"To smell good. By the way, that suit you have on is impeccable."

"It's Tom Ford, and I thought you were going to be honest."

"Fine." She rolled her eyes. "I bought it because yes, I *have* been seeing a new man. His name is Anthony Castillo. He's a security guard at the bank down the block." She set a few more fresh napkins next to my drink. "Let me know what the background check says." She winked.

"Yes, ma'am."

"And really, Roman, you don't need to be so protective of me."

When I didn't respond, she changed tack. "So. How many will be joining you tonight?"

"Just one."

"Yes, sir." Francisca leaned in, poured the whiskey into the glass, and whispered, "Someone met the senator earlier, in the hallway by the bathrooms. A tall, balding man wearing a navy suit over a white dress shirt. An American. He was alone—didn't order anything. Left promptly after. I tried to get a look at the car but missed it. If he comes back, I'll be watching, and I'll get the license plate."

"Did they exchange anything?"

"Only words."

"You're sure?"

"One hundred percent."

"Thank you, Francisca."

She nodded, then disappeared into the kitchen.

I sipped, eyeing the crowd over the rim of my glass, settling on the senator who'd recently traveled to a small seaside town where a large human-trafficking sale went down. It was a loose connection, but one worth investigating nonetheless, especially considering he frequented my bar.

"Roman."

My attention shifted to the six-foot-seven monster in a brown suit approaching from the side. Always from the side.

"Kieran." I stood.

We shook hands as Francisca returned and poured another glass of whiskey.

"The bar is crazy tonight," Kieran said as he settled into the booth.

His Irish accent was almost undetectable. While Kieran had intentionally suppressed his accent after moving to the States and joining the CIA, I'd clutched onto mine with bloody fingernails. It was who I was, and I feared losing that part of me would derail my focus.

Kieran picked up his highball and sipped, then swallowed. His brows arched as he eyed the amber liquid. "Nice."

"The senator brought it over for you."

"I'll bet he did." Kieran smirked and leaned his elbows on the table.

Although it had been two years since I'd last seen him, the forty-something looked the exact same. Short auburn hair combed to the side, and a perfectly trimmed beard, colored to match.

Kieran Healy was the only man to ever beat me at arm wrestling—something he still reminds me of to this day. We'd met shortly after I began working for Astor Stone, a paramilitary contracting firm operating under the guise of a private investigation firm. Both being Irish immigrants, we'd bonded quickly, forming a strong working relationship, and the closest thing to a friendship I had.

Allowed for, anyway.

"Too bad he didn't bring over one of his women too," Kieran said.

"I thought you learned your lesson with the last one."

"I learned to lock up my wallet before the clothes come off." He shrugged. "Fun night, though. Worth every damn second."

"Not many people would consider getting mugged a good night."

"Not many people can bend the way she could." He smirked. "Speaking of—you got a woman yet?"

"One that won't steal my money? No."

"Think about it. You're not getting any younger. One day, you'll regret dying alone."

"I'll be dying. I won't care."

"*Alone.* Alone is the point. You'll be dying *alone.*"

I grabbed a napkin that I didn't need and wiped at a spot on the table that wasn't there.

Kieran grinned. "So, what time did you get in?"

"About four hours ago."

"How long have you been in Mexico?"

"Less than two weeks."

"Puerto Vallarta?"

I nodded.

"Find anything yet?"

"Not a fucking thing. I'm heading back in a few hours— have a meeting tomorrow with an undercover agent with the Mexican government. Now, what do you have for me?" I asked, getting to the point. I despised small talk almost as much as Mexican caviar.

"I have ten minutes to catch up with an old friend and drink some stolen whiskey."

"Come on—"

"Dude, you know I could get fired, maybe even killed, for meeting you under the radar like this."

"And I know you're fucking the daughter of the Mexican ambassador to the US. So, unless you want this information to run in the morning paper . . ."

"God, you're a dick."

"Which is why we get along so well."

"Sadly, true. Okay. First off, the anonymous email that was sent to you with the video is totally untraceable."

"Why?"

"Whoever sent it used a fake IP address and ghost server. Impossible to trace. Same with the video attached. It was an altered file."

"So what?"

"So, when a file gets edited, it erases the original metadata."

I lifted my drink. "You didn't come here to tell me you failed, Kieran."

"I don't fail. As I said, the video you sent me was altered —edited for an effect on a cell phone app. This didn't surprise me, considering the content, but what did is that the location had been altered as well."

I frowned.

"Let me explain," he said. "Cell phones use location services to pinpoint your location, using a combination of GPS, Bluetooth, hot spots, and cell tower locations."

"Geotagging. Get to the fucking point."

"Right. So, every time you take a photo or video, a whole bunch of information is captured as EXIF data as part of the metadata. This data tells me a shit-load of stuff, like not only when, where, and how the video or communication was conducted, but also who else was involved, who initi- ated the communication, etc. But thanks to the uproar in privacy issues, phone manufacturers have added options for users to remove the location metadata, making it a hell of a lot harder for people like me to track, and easier for bad guys to get away with shit . . . especially when they become crafty."

"Define crafty."

"It's called spoofing, or schema poisoning. Basically, in this instance, instead of turning off their location services, whoever sent the video to you spoofed the metadata by assigning a fake location to the file."

"To throw me off."

"Right."

"Which means whoever sent the video has something to hide and knows he's being tracked."

"No doubt about it. The intention can be not only to mislead trackers, but throw off an investigation, or even blackmail." Kieran sipped his drink. "Or they could just be fucking with you."

"Someone doesn't send a video of a kidnapped woman collared and chained just for laughs."

Kieran shrugged, unaffected. The man had seen it all.

"So, that's it?" I said. "That's all you got for me?"

"I'd say that confirming that someone is fucking with you, and probably watching your every move, is information worth delivering."

"Thanks."

"Someone doesn't want you investigating this missing girl case."

"Someone doesn't want her found. It's got nothing to do with me."

"You sure about that?" he asked.

No, I wasn't, but spitballing conspiracy theories wasn't the point of the visit.

"So," he said, "is the video of her? Of the missing American girl?"

"No. It's of another victim that was recently abducted from a luxury Mexican resort. A local girl kidnapped exactly fourteen days ago, the same day the American girl went missing. The authorities believe the same group kidnapped three women that night."

"The Cussane Network."

"Right."

"It's been two weeks and *you* still haven't found her?"

I shifted in my seat.

Kieran laughed. "So *that's* why you called me. You're desperate."

"Not desperate enough to sleep with the ambassador's daughter."

Kieran's laughter faded, and for a second, I wondered if he had real feelings for the girl. An interesting thought about a man almost as coldhearted as I was.

"Okay, so let's back up here," he said, avoiding the quip. "The US government hired you to find the girl, right?"

"Yes and no."

"Feels like this should be very black and white."

"Things are never black and white. They hired the company I work for, Astor Stone, Inc., but only because they believe she might know where something is that is very valuable to them."

"Valuable to the US government?"

And me.

Kieran nodded as he sipped. "So, your mission isn't really to save her, it's to gather intel from her. Do they have proof she's alive?"

"No."

"Do you?"

"No."

"Okay . . ." Kieran narrowed his eyes and settled back against the seat. "Now tell me why you're lying to me."

"What makes you think I'm lying?"

"Because I know they officially declared the missing American girl dead *yesterday*, which means they've dropped her case—and you've been dropped too."

In her ever-perfect timing, Francisca breezed up to the table, refilled my drink, then topped off Kieran's.

After she disappeared again, he continued. "But you haven't dropped it. Why are you still searching for this girl? Or more importantly, why do you think she's still alive?"

I cocked a brow. "Want to come with me, K? Help me out?"

"No."

"Then quit asking so many goddamn questions."

Kieran continued to press—his best and worst quality. "But you obviously think she's still alive, so that means this is some grand *save the girl, save the world* opportunity to you."

"Save the girl, take down an entire human-trafficking network, which will lead to another, and another, and another . . ."

Kieran regarded me closely. Too closely. "Have you ever thought about doing anything with your life other than toeing the thin line between good and evil?"

"Undercover work isn't pretty."

"Neither is hell, bro."

A white-hot spark popped on the back of my neck. "What the fuck is that supposed to mean?"

"It means, I know many men—*good* agents—who went undercover for too long, like you. Lost themselves along the way. Did things that they should have never done, *didn't* do things they *should have* done, all in the name of the job. Thing is, with you, it's not the job—it's more, and that's when it gets dicey." He pointed his drink at me. "And let me tell you something. You need to be on-fucking-point when dealing with the CUN, brother."

"You don't know shit about me, Kieran."

"I know enough to know that you didn't just decide to dedicate your life to saving women from the sex trade because you're a good guy. There's something else driving you, and if you're not careful, it's going to consume you." He stared at me a minute. "They don't know you're continuing the case, do they?"

"Define they."

"The US government."

"No."

"Your boss?"

"No."

"So, you've just gone totally rogue to find this chick." Kieran shook his head and laughed. "Jesus, man, you're going to get yourself killed."

When I didn't respond, he tapped his fingers on the table, emphasizing his point made, then stood.

"Don't forget, Roman, everything you do leaves a trace. And speaking of that, leave me out of it from here on out. You're on your own—although, I have a feeling that's exactly where you prefer to be." He tipped back the last of his whiskey. "Happy hunting, my friend."

I watched Kieran weave through the crowd. Once he'd disappeared into the night, I laid ten one-hundred-dollar bills on the table and slipped out of the booth.

I had a plane to catch.

6

ROMAN

*R*ipping the tie from my neck, I stepped onto the sidewalk and into the balmy, humid air. I tossed the noose onto the cobblestone street, watching it fall like dead weight into a puddle littered with cigarette butts.

There was no breeze in this city.

The fucking heat. It was one of the many things I never got used to in Mexico, along with the noise, the crowds, the clogged air, and the smell of urine baking on the asphalt.

Mariachi and hip-hop music blared from the bars that lined the street, shouts and laughter echoing from the apartments overhead. Street vendors crowded the sidewalks, selling a little of this and a little of that. Bikes and scooters zipped past, deftly weaving between locals and tourists alike.

Whether male or female, rich or poor, everyone was searching for something that night. Most eventually would find it at the bottom of a bottle.

I noticed a group of teenagers exchange a small bag of drugs in an alley next to a pair of dumpsters spray-painted with gang signs. Twenty feet away, two prostitutes watched with keen interest. One feverishly scratching the scabs on her face, the other wild-eyed, bouncing from heel to heel.

The economy in this part of the city was thriving.

I watched the drug deal go down, and before the dealers were even out of sight, the prostitutes descended on their targets. Down the block, a few more hookers emerged, smelling blood in the water. I watched this shameless exchange for goods and services as I strode down the street in my four-thousand-dollar suit and two-thousand-dollar shoes.

I thought of the circular flow of money. The domino effect one transaction has on another, and how eventually, habits and societies are formed around this flow. It's an endless, and sometimes very vicious, cycle.

In this case, money is paid to the drug dealers for their product. That money is then given to the hookers who were waiting to strike. The prostitutes use their payment to buy more drugs from the drug dealer, who, in turn, uses the money to make more drugs to sell to more kids on the street. And on and on we go.

Then there are the men and women the government pays to police this thriving economic subset, though not nearly enough to justify a full dedication of self to the job. These men and women are a very different type of people, using their paycheck as a means of survival to pay for food, homes, cars, college tuition, and so on. There is no passion in what they do. They work because this is what society tells them they need to do. They live within the acceptable standards of human existence, and that is all.

The drug dealers, on the other hand? The buyers? The prostitutes? They live and breathe for their payments, for their products. Their entire world revolves around getting another hit. Not food, not water, not college tuition. For them, it's another high, whether by drugs or orgasm.

Addiction, greed, lust, or power . . . it consumes them. This subset of the economy operates on passion, that carnal need to sate desires of the flesh. They buy, sell, and trade a *feeling*. And this is why they win.

This is why they'll always win.

I watched the hookers lead the kids around the corner and disappear into the darkness.

A sudden slideshow of images flashed in my head. Women, girls, bloodied, beaten within an inch of their life. Chained to walls, locked in cages. The sound of their screams echoed in my head, along with the shouts, the crack of the whips.

I felt my pulse kick, adrenaline awakening in my veins.

Pulling in a sharp breath, I shook the visions from my head, and once again was annoyed that I pictured them at all. And worse than that, that they made me *feel*.

Kieran's words whispered through my ear. *". . . didn't do things they should have done . . ."*

I nodded at the doorman as I stepped into the glass high-rise that housed my latest property. My mind was preoccupied during the ride on the elevator, the walk down the long corridor, and finally, the turning of the key to my apartment.

I flicked on the light as I kicked the door closed with my heel.

Framed in the floor-to-ceiling window ahead of me, the moon hung low above the city, which sparkled with energy and life. My wingtips clicked against the marble floors, echoing off the empty walls as I strode to the window.

Stripping out of my suit jacket, I stared down onto the streets.

The real estate agent had sold me hard on the view. And yes, I suppose it was a beautiful view. But all I saw was the hookers in the shadows, the drug dealers, the gangs, the secrets, the lies. The death.

My gaze refocused on the reflection of the penthouse suite behind me, the place that I would call home for six months a year.

The black-and-white marble floor gleamed, the walls a patent black, the kitchen, sparkling lines of every upscale appliance known to man. But not a single stick of furniture.

"You're gonna regret dying alone . . ."

I turned, glancing at the double doors that led into the master bedroom. A king-size mattress lay on the floor, next to a closet full of designer suits and a safe packed with guns and money.

Money that went to shady places, guns that went into even shadier hands.

"Even the good ones get lost . . ."

"Fuck you, Kieran," I mumbled.

I stalked to the kitchen, beelining it to the bottle of whiskey I kept within easy access. After pouring a glass, I centered myself over the collage of reports, maps, and photos that littered the counter.

Seven days.

I glanced at the clock.

I had seven days to find Samantha Greene.

Was I desperate? Yeah. Kieran didn't know the half of it, including what would happen when the seven days were up.

Feeling abnormally on edge, I sifted through the papers, though I didn't need to. I'd memorized her file like the back of my hand.

Days after Samantha had been reported missing, the US government received a number of tips on her disappearance, including information that Samantha had been kidnapped by a ruthless cartel known as the CUN Network. If the tips were true, I knew from gathering my own intel that Samantha would be included in a group of slaves that were to be shipped overseas to a massive auction where they would be sold like cattle—*in seven days*.

Another tip suggested that while in captivity, Samantha had been chosen and positioned as the CUN leader's personal slave and possibly future wife.

While the first tip was the most troubling, the latter presented a unique opportunity. Samantha's access to the leader of the CUN Network gave her unique insight into the leader's business dealings, including a USB drive that could bring down a worldwide slavery network.

And this was when finding Samantha Greene became the US government's number one priority.

Because of the delicate dance of working with the widely corrupt Mexican government, the DOD contacted the company that I worked for, Astor Stone, Inc., which was contracted to help aid in her search. I was requested specifically.

After all, no one knew the industry like I did, and no one had the contacts that I had, especially in that area.

That day, I accepted the mission, packed my bags, and caught the next flight out to Oklahoma, where I learned everything I could about Samantha Greene. Then on to Puerto Vallarta, where I re-entered the dark underworld of human slavery.

I'd expected to be in and out in a matter of hours.

How wrong I was.

Days of chasing my fucking tail later, Samantha's bones were found on the outskirts of a remote village in the Sierra Madre Mountains. No one in the village had reported seeing her or anyone suspicious—though they wouldn't tell me if they had.

Samantha Greene was officially declared dead by the US government and her case was closed, along with any hope of finding the USB drive.

This is where the story of many missing women end. News of the deceased is delivered to the family. Tears are shed, funerals are held, lives are changed forever. This is where the women become memories, soon to fade into nothing more than the cold black lines of a human trafficking statistic. Soon to be completely forgotten by everyone.

Everyone except me.

Kieran was right. I'd been officially dropped from the case. He was also correct that I was stubborn.

I didn't believe Samantha was dead, because unfortunately, I knew this story all too well—the real story, I should say. I knew that most of the time, human remains are used as a diversion. Teeth or bones are extracted from the victims, then planted in indiscriminate locations to throw off investigations.

You see, if someone is considered dead, there's no reason to continue searching for them. The planted bones are intended to erase the victim from society and resurrect them as an identity-less product to be sold and traded for profit. These once active, "normal" members of society become modern-day slaves, forced by torture, fraud, or coercion to engage in commercial sex.

The world has labeled them as dead. However, in reality, the victim is still alive, living a horrific life that only few can imagine.

Seasoning, as it is called, is phase one of the breaking down of the slave. This process serves to recalibrate what the slave once considered life, or freedom. Traffickers use a combination of psychological manipulation, intimidation, gang rape, sodomy, torture, deprivation of food or sleep, isolation, drugs, and threatening or holding hostage something dear to the victim to control them.

The process typically lasts for weeks, for the stronger-willed sometimes longer. The victims are kept in cages, assigned numbers, given dog collars, and treated like animals.

After being seasoned, the victims are transported to various locations around the world to be sold and traded like cattle at a livestock auction. Some are sold to individuals, some to other trafficking groups, and some are sold into organ harvesting—something that I won't go into here.

Samantha was just one of three women taken in Puerto Vallarta that night, one of twenty-one million victims sold into slavery worldwide, a global business of $150 billion. It's one of the largest issues facing humanity today. An industry that is primarily run by a rapidly expanding global cartel, one that I had an intimate relationship with.

The Cussane Network (the CUN) was started in Ireland, my homeland, in the late 1970s as a drug cartel. After quickly earning a reputation for their brutal coercion tactics, the CUN expanded into firearms dealing and smuggling, and then into human trafficking, quickly monopolizing the Irish black market. In 1981, the organization branched out to Mexico, where they laid roots, capitalizing on the corrupt political system.

The leader of the CUN was a man named Conor Cussane, son of its founder, Oisin Cussane. While Oisin had been the face of the organization, posing for more than a hundred photos that appeared in the media over the course of his reign, his son, Conor, had been nothing more than a phantom since he took over after his father's death, ruling the group with an iron fist from behind a wall of protection.

Rumored to rarely leave his South American beachfront mansion, Conor gained the reputation of a brown recluse spider—just as elusive, and just as deadly. This exclusivity, combined with whispers of his rumored good looks, created a sort of mystical allure around him, making him idolized by young and old thugs alike. Some even considered Conor an actual god with supernatural powers.

But, as we know from every Greek tale ever told, every god has a weakness.

Conor's weakness lay in the USB drive he carried with him—*on him*—at all times. This drive contained a list of every man, woman, terrorist, head of state, president, senator, governor, priest, and/or chief of police who had ever purchased a drug, gun, or human from the CUN, or had been involved in any way. It was rumored that the list contained the date, time, and location of every transaction on the list. Conor used it for blackmail.

It was, without question, a list that could singlehandedly take down a billion-dollar industry, save millions of lives, and bring closure to thousands of families.

The thing was, Conor Cussane lived almost in total isolation, with only a select few of the most sinister and trustworthy criminals allowed to see him and bear witness to his business dealings. It was rumored that only a dozen people had met the man face-to-face.

Soon to be thirteen.

For fourteen months, I'd been working undercover to help the CUN breach the US border. I'd divulged confidential information, forged paperwork, and laundered money, each questionable undertaking bringing me one step closer to being allowed behind the iron curtain.

Finally, I got my chance.

After securing a transport of slaves into Texas, I received a call from one of Conor's closest business associates informing me of Conor's interest in me becoming part of the leadership of the US branch of his business. He requested a meet. I invited him to one of my private residences, offering extended use of the lodge by his men.

I was in.

I'd worked my entire life for this—for coming face-to-face with Conor Cussane. The son of the man who'd killed my mother. The man who carried a single object that could save thousands of lives.

I was so *damn* close.

The missing American, Samantha Greene, provided the perfect opportunity. She would give me the insight and intel I needed to locate the USB, and I'd save her in the process.

Two birds with one stone.

Problem is, the clock was ticking. In seven days, Samantha and the rest of the slaves would be transported overseas.

Seven days to find Samantha, get the USB, and avenge my mother.

Yes, Samantha Greene was my mission, but *Conor Cussane* was my target.

7

ROMAN

*K*nowing sleep would evade me, I poured another glass of whiskey, pushed aside the file I knew too well, and grabbed the stack of mail piled on the counter.

Bills, bills, more bills, solicitations.

I ripped open the manila envelope that contained the mail forwarded from my house in the States, next door to Astor Stone's headquarters in an inconspicuous small town called Berry Springs.

Bills, bills . . .

I tossed the stack aside, opened my laptop, and clicked into my multiple email accounts. My fingers froze on the keyboard.

Another one.

With a sigh, I clicked into the email.

Roman, hi. It's me again. I hope all is well. I would love to hear from you.
I plan to send you your mother's things this week. I've had them

in a box in my closet for nearly thirty years now, as you already know if you've read any one of the dozens of emails I've sent over the years. I don't know if you're even getting these messages, or if you care for that matter, but I truly feel like the last of your mother's belongings should go to you. I believe she would have wanted this.

Please let me know as soon as possible where to send them.

— Freya Doyle

I clicked the DELETE button. Grabbing my drink, I downed the contents in one go.

I turned, then strode into the bedroom and into the closet to pack a bag of clean clothes. My flight back to Puerto Vallarta was scheduled to leave at five in the morning. Once that was done, I poured another drink and settled on the floor, leaning against the window frame.

Sipping slowly now, I stared down onto the city, as I did every night. I wondered how the prostitutes had fared through their exchange. I wondered if they were high now, surrounded by needles, finally happy and content.

Finally, I pulled the picture from my pocket. The edges were worn, the corner ripped. I stared at the blond hair, the wide hazel eyes, and the smile that could light a room.

Samantha Greene.

I thought of my mother. She had that kind of smile. Sighing, I rested my head against the window frame.

When will it all end?

Soon.

Soon, I promised myself.

Soon.

*T*he sun tricked me that morning.

Thick cloud cover blanketed the sky outside the hopper window, dimming the early morning light. The basement was dark and bleak, but still hot as sin.

I missed the sun that morning, oddly so. It was a little piece of normalcy, a reminder of the world that lay outside my captivity.

The brunette had been returned sometime during the night. Locked in her cage, she hadn't moved since, probably still knocked out from whatever drugs they'd given her.

The smell of coffee wafted down from the rusty vents. I closed my eyes and inhaled, momentarily swept back to my leather couch and tattered blanket.

You'd think after weeks of not having a drop of caffeine, the craving would subside.

Nope.

Every morning—every *single* morning—my captors brewed coffee. Some days, the smell would be so strong, I assumed they were brewing it on top of the floor vents, just to fuck with us. A silly thought. Regardless, every morning, the scent alone made my mouth water, a flurry of sorrow igniting in me seconds later.

Coffee. God, I missed it. I missed the ritual of it. I missed my couch, my blanket, my dog. I missed the hope that came with each new day.

It's going to be a good day, I would tell myself every morning after the buzz of the caffeine kicked in. And dammit, I would do everything I could to make it a good day. I'd remind myself how lucky I was to have a job that I loved, a car that got me from point A to point B, students who meant the world to me. A mother who meant more.

Fucking coffee. I would have killed for a cup that morning.

I noticed increased movement across the floors overhead. Loud, excited voices, which was abnormal for that time of day. Something was happening, I could feel it in my bones.

I began to grow nervous, listening to—*feeling*, rather— the sense of urgency upstairs.

I stared at the ceiling, wondering what the fuss was about. What the random bangs were, the orders being shouted in Spanish.

Just then, the basement door opened.

Capitán clomped down the steps, wearing his usual army fatigues and black boots, followed by one of his minions. Another followed, then another.

My instinct that something was about to happen skyrocketed. I looked at the brunette, still asleep, then back at the men.

There was a sudden and very noticeable shift in the room. It was fear, I realized—and not only from me.

Capitán ordered the men, pointing around the room. The guards scattered, checking this, checking that, picking up this and that. They whispered back and forth.

I caught the name *Ardri.*

The word was familiar to me, and not just because I'd heard it a few times already. Ardri had been a character in one of the fairy tales I'd read as a little girl. The word translated to *high king.*

The basement door opened.

A black figure—all black—stepped into the room, a massive, ominous silhouette backlit by the hallway. Black hair, black suit, and a pair of shiny black wingtips that probably cost more than my car. A black shadow over a face that somehow gave me chills.

Tap, one step, *tap*, another. Even the sound of his heels against the concrete was intimidating.

The guards snapped into line, straightening like soldiers greeting the president.

I was bewildered, wondering who could make these evil, seemingly fearless men act like subservient little boys with nothing but the click of his shoe?

One of the guards cleared his throat, glaring at me.

I quickly looked down, immediately regretting not chancing a peek at the face of the man who had turned Capitán compliant. There was no question the man who entered the room was someone of great importance.

The King. I was sure I hadn't come into contact with him before.

Who was he?

I watched Capitán and the guards stride across the room, single file. Hands were shaken, pleasantries exchanged, and again, I heard the man addressed as Ardri.

Then he spoke. His voice was low and deep, with a terrifying authority that cut like glass. He spoke in Spanish, but his voice carried a strong Irish lilt.

Something tickled in my stomach.

The guards listened intently as the King spoke, as did I, trying to discern what was going on.

Attention shifted to the brunette on the floor, now awake, trembling against the back of her cage. It appeared that Capitán was relaying the details of his latest slave to the man in black.

Then all attention pivoted to me. I could feel *his* gaze on me before he even took a single step. My heart thundered as the King crossed the room, the others close on his heels.

An unfamiliar scent caught in the breeze from the fan. A fresh, clean, citrusy scent. Happy, like my childhood. I was pulled back there, into the past, for just a moment. Pulled back to freedom.

Something awoke deep inside me with that scent alone.
Freedom.

Suddenly, distant screams broke the silence. Two voices, two harrowing cries, drawing closer and closer to the basement door.

The hair on the back of my neck stood on end. I wondered what the hell was going on.

Capitán said something to the King, to which he didn't respond.

The guards turned away from me as the door opened. Keeping my head down, I peeked under my lashes.

With my limited field of vision, I couldn't see the two newcomers dragged past me, only their shoes. One wore a pair of white Converse with pink soles, and the other, black-and-red basketball sneakers.

Without considering the consequences, I looked up, the quiet now shattered by the piercing, blood-curdling screams of a young girl. Next to her was a young boy. They were twins, as best I could tell. Both were no more than age ten or twelve, about the same age as the children I taught in school.

No.

Oh my God was all I could think. A weird motherly instinct ignited like fire inside me. They were too young to be in a hellhole like this. Much too young.

The girl was wearing a pink tank top and a pair of denim shorts. The boy, a collared blue golf shirt and khaki shorts. They looked like every student I'd ever taught.

My brain was telling me to turn away, but desperation and panic kept my focus trained on the children.

Capitán said something to the King. Again, this was met with no response. The children were dragged across the floor.

Had the King brought the children? Did they belong to him?

The boy vomited all over himself, the floor, and the boots of the man next to him. Chaos ensued. The girl attempted to fight the men, to defend her brother, sick with fear.

Tears welled in my eyes.

Screaming, the children were shoved into separate cages. The girl continued to fight, trying to get to her brother. It was a horrific scene.

Unable to take it, I closed my eyes and covered my ears, focusing on the muted whirl of that goddamn fan.

My body began to tremble.

I squeezed my eyes shut, trying to retreat to the "happy

place" I'd created since becoming a slave of human trafficking. I imagined everything fading away around me like smoke on the wind. The screams, the darkness, the heat, the smell, the men, the girls, the cages.

I inhaled and exhaled as lyrics slowly filtered into my head.

Somewhere over the rainbow . . .

Inhaled, exhaled.

Bluebirds fly . . .

I heard my mother's voice, pulling me back to when she used to sing to me while tucking me in bed. I envisioned fluffy white clouds against a sapphire-blue sky, the bright, happy colors of the rainbow. In my head, I sang it over and over until the screaming stopped, and I heard the deafening thud of two bodies falling like dead weight onto the floor.

The children had been drugged.

I dropped my hands from my ears, exhaling in relief, grateful that the kids were no longer awake to feel the fear, see the horror around them.

Leaving the children, the guards stepped to the brunette's cage. I lowered my head once again.

A moment passed as words were exchanged between the men, but nothing from the man in black. He'd gone silent the moment the children were brought into the room.

I listened to footsteps cross the floor, the clink of the wire cutters being plucked from their rusty hook in the wall.

A tear escaped my eye. No amount of meditation could take away what was going to happen next.

I listened to the sound of the cage being opened. Heard the shuffle as the sedated brunette was pulled to a seated position.

I heard her scream.

Heard the pop of bone as her finger was removed.

Heard the wails, the pleas, and the sobs that followed as she was shoved back into her cage and locked inside.

The guards turned.

Not the children, I prayed, *not the children.*

Instead, my cage door was opened.

"*Venir*," Capitán barked.

I obeyed, slowly crawling forward like a dog, my head down, scanning the floor as far as I could see. A pair of black wingtips next to black combat boots.

When I reached the front of my cage, Capitán crouched before me, painfully gripped my chin, and yanked my face upward. I tensed, expecting a blow from either him or the King.

But nothing came. Instead, the King said something to Capitán, and again my ears perked at his deep Irish brogue.

"Open your eyes," Capitán demanded of me in broken English.

I didn't.

My hair was fisted, my head viciously jerked, sending a shot of pain up the back of my neck.

"Open your eyes," he snapped, jerking my hair again. "Look at him."

Him—the King.

Squinting, I slowly opened my eyes, still expecting some sort of physical attack. Instead, I was met with a pair of slitted emerald-green irises staring at me so intently, I was jarred by the moment.

My stomach flipped in some sort of immediate visceral reaction to him. His face was hard, sharp lines carved from granite, his hair as black as a raven's wing, his body as tall and thick as a mountain.

He was absolutely terrifying, but in the most gorgeous, drop-to-your-knees sexy way.

I took all of him in—the designer suit, the expensive gold watch around his wrist, the poise in his squared shoulders, the power in his stance, the unnerving dominance that came as naturally to him as breathing. A man of generational wealth, I would have guessed, if not for the jagged scar above his eyebrow and the tattoo licking up the side of his neck.

The King dipped his chin in some sort of approval of me.

Capitán shoved my face away, releasing my hair.

Like a magnet, my pulse roaring, I locked eyes with the King. *Take me*, I mentally begged in some sort of completely irrational desperation. *Take me away from here.*

Surely, this man had a nice home. He wasn't dirty and gross like the men I'd been enslaved to. I could be his—he didn't seem that bad.

This is what I was thinking at that moment. *This* is how the fucked-up mind of a slave works, twisted by imprisonment.

It was already happening. They were brainwashing me. There I was, secretly begging to be sold to the man they called the King, instead of begging for freedom. I'd take ease where I could find it, like a dog begging for scraps from a table.

It made me sick.

Our gazes lingered before the King turned his back to me. I couldn't fight the withering feeling of rejection.

I listened to his steps as he walked away, the guards following like dogs on a leash.

The door opened, the men filed out, and the door slammed shut again. The locks slid into place.

I looked at the brunette as she held her mutilated hand

to her chest and sobbed on the floor, then at the children, merely unconscious heaps in their cages.

The tiny window was still dark with clouds. There were no rainbows here.

I was a fool.

With that thought, I bowed my head and began to weep.

9

ROMAN

I stared at Capitán, his mouth moving, hands gesturing, though I had no idea what the man was saying. My thoughts were still in the basement, still frozen in time from when my brain had short-circuited the moment I laid eyes on Samantha Greene lying at the bottom of a cage.

I'd finally found her—and she was staggeringly beautiful.

Despite the cuts, the bruises, the grime and dirt, Samantha Greene was stunning, or in spite of them, perhaps. A beauty so rare that cameras were unable to capture it.

It had taken everything I had in me not to rip off Capitán's hand when he gripped that long blond hair and yanked that delicate face.

It wasn't the first time I'd seen men treat a woman like that. But it was the first time—*ever*—that I'd had a reaction, a visceral surge of protectiveness, that it almost crippled me, almost destroyed my cover and everything I'd worked for.

She appeared even younger than in her pictures. I'm

sure to her that I, the King as they called me, appeared even older than forty-two years. A nasty old man paying for sex, she'd probably thought, hating me as much as the other men.

This bothered me, and *that* bothered me.

I blinked, trying to focus on the moment, on the bastard in front of me who I had to pretend to respect. Trying to remind myself of the real reason I was there.

The reason that had nothing to do with the blond-haired goddess in the basement.

*T*he next day passed like the ones before it. Long hours of hot, humid darkness, broken up by discarded scraps of disgusting food and water that tasted like dirt.

Capitán had sent someone to stitch up the brunette's mutilated hand. She'd finally quit crying, realizing it was safer to fade into the shadows and remain quiet and still.

I was grateful for this.

The children had been removed from the room, the guards taking whatever was left of my soul along with them. I stared at the basement door for hours, awaiting their return.

It never came.

The guilt I felt for not fighting to save them when they were dragged in was more painful, more sickening, than anything I'd felt since being kidnapped.

They were *children*. Beautiful, innocent, naive little beings of wonder.

As a teacher, I knew far too well how a child's environment can mold their personality. I knew that every life experience was shaping who they would become, the paths they would choose. At the beginning of each school year, I could pinpoint the children who lived in warm, happy, wholesome households, and those who lived under loveless, selfish rule.

I read an article once about children who faced mental and/or physical abuse before their brains were fully developed enough to compartmentalize the experience. The effects went far beyond emotional, to actually changing the brain's physiological makeup. As a result of the abuse, the children live in a constant state of fight or flight, never being taught how to rationalize, calm themselves, and deal with such anxieties. Therefore, complex personalities are developed, curating abnormal—or incorrect—responses to stimuli.

To put it plainly, this is the recipe for severe personality disorders. Serial killers, rapists, and kids who shoot up schools often suffer personality disorders created by early childhood circumstance.

What would this experience do to the children? To their fragile little minds? How would this mold them? It's unfair, and in most cases preventable.

Except I didn't prevent it. I didn't do a damn thing to help those children but close my eyes and selfishly praying to escape.

The brunette stirred in her cage, something startling her awake. Our eyes met just as I registered what she'd heard— footsteps outside the basement door.

I lifted my finger to my lips, reminding her to be quiet and stay still. She nodded.

The door opened and a flood of guards piled in, a sense of urgency in their step, hyperawareness in their beady black eyes.

I recognized most of the men, but noted a few new faces as well.

We were told to stay quiet and to do exactly as they said, or they would kill us.

The doors of our cages were opened. We were pulled to our feet, our hands cuffed at our stomachs. We were told to keep our eyes shut and heads down, and then, with guns in our faces, we were shuffled out of the room. It was the first time I'd been allowed out of the basement since being taken.

We were marched single file into a dark hallway that smelled of coffee, cigarettes, pot, and the musty scent of an old window air-conditioning unit. The cool air stunned my heated skin, instantly cooling the blue housedress I'd been given, and that's when I realized the fabric was moist with sweat. I felt a rush of embarrassment, of shame at how I must look and smell.

The stained linoleum felt cool against my bare feet, and I wiggled my toes, trying to rid them of the sweat and dirt that was surely between them.

The guards spoke quickly, and there were more of them than usual in the house, I could tell. Something big was definitely happening.

I wondered if the King had anything to do with this sudden change of routine. It only made sense that he did.

Keeping my head down, I peeked under my lashes, searching for any sign of the children. No luck.

I took in every detail of our prison, mentally cataloging every item, color, and sound, in case I needed to relay the information to the police at some point. In case I ever got out—no—*when* I got out.

The flooring was old, the rooms furnished with only the necessities. It appeared to be a regular low-income house.

By the lack of decor, I deduced that this was no family home. This building served a purpose. This house existed solely to hold slaves.

I could hear cars passing by and horns tapping in the distance. I realized that we were being held somewhere in town, somewhere in civilization—not in an abandoned warehouse in the middle of nowhere, like most abduction movies depict.

The house was in the middle of a freaking neighborhood, and this absolutely stupefied me.

How could this kind of thing happen in the open?

How many homes in this neighborhood held prisoners?

How many of *your* neighbors harbor deadly secrets?

How close are you to being able to save someone?

Would you know the signs of human trafficking if you saw it?

With each step, memories of the day I was taken began to form, broken moments here and there, murky flashbacks of being dragged across this same linoleum.

Had I screamed? Had a neighbor heard and simply shrugged it off?

The thought sickened me.

We were led outside into a hot, sticky night. I sucked in the briny ocean air, imagining it cleansing my lungs of the stink of the basement.

It happened so quickly, I didn't have time to react. The brunette jerked out of the men's hold and sprinted at the first scent of freedom.

She was shot three times in the back, the silenced bullets thudding into her body.

I heard her last gasp of air. Heard her body hit the ground.

I turned my face as I was marched past her dead body,

holding my breath so as not to smell the blood pouring from her. My heart roared as I forced my gaze to stay on my dirty bare feet. One step, another, and another.

The grind of doors opening sounded ahead, the smell of oil and gasoline wafting on the air. Though I couldn't hear them, I could feel that I was suddenly in the presence of many people. My heart beat faster.

"Up."

The backs of my bare legs were whipped by a stick, the gun shoved into the side of my head as I approached what appeared to be the back of a U-Haul truck, the kind of inconspicuous moving van you pass every day on the highway without giving it a second glance. Most are filled with food or cargo, but this one was filled with at least a dozen slaves of human trafficking. Each was handcuffed, barely dressed, covered in bruises, sitting in rows on the floor.

I could feel the fear radiating off them.

What is happening? Where are we being taken?

I struggled to get up into the truck, not only because my hands were cuffed but because my legs were stiff from being immobile for weeks.

"Up!" the guard spat in my face.

I scrambled onto the trailer, accidently slamming my knee as I pulled my leg up to meet my body. Someone laughed behind me.

A hand gripped my bicep, jerking me for my incompetence. Then I was pulled to my feet and guided down the row of skinny, desensitized humans.

That's when I saw them. Four wide, wild eyes among the dead souls. The children, barely visible behind two adult women.

I stumbled, shifting my body weight as I slipped out of

the hands of my captor and fell onto the floor, scrambling my way to the children. Someone screamed. The guards yelled, guns lifted.

I slid behind the children, pulled my knees to my chest, and froze, keeping my eyes down.

My life was spared that night.

Once the doors were shut and secured, we were told by the guards who remained in the trailer to stay down, stay quiet, and to not move. Wearing army fatigues and balaclavas, and carrying AK-47s, they walked through the rows of slaves, tapping our heads with the tip of the barrel as they passed. Up and down, up and down, they slowly walked through the rows of slaves.

We drove for hours upon hours through that night.

The little boy was deathly pale, his skin gray, his eyes glassy. This time, he threw up quietly in his hand and hid it there. I began to wonder if he had some sort of sickness. An illness that needed medication.

At some point, we were given water to drink and some sort of wafers to eat.

Over the course of the ride, I noticed the girl becoming increasingly agitated in front of me, shifting constantly, breathing heavily, an occasional moan escaping her chapped lips. I didn't know what was happening until she shifted enough to where I noticed the blood smeared on the floor. The girl had started her period. For the first time, I guessed.

I recalled the first time I'd started my period. I was in the bathroom, my mom next to me, boxes of both pads and tampons laid out in front of me—because my mom didn't know which brand I would like the most, so she'd bought them all. We went through it together, she and I.

The girl's shoulders shook as she began to cry.

My heart shattered.

I gently put my hand on her back, staring for a moment at the grotesque deformity that had once been my pinky finger.

I closed my eyes, bowed my head, and began to pray.

11

SAM

*W*hen the U-Haul came to an abrupt stop, I awoke with a jolt. Bodies banged against each other, unceremoniously awoken. Wide, panicked eyes gazed back and forth, everyone curious as to where we had arrived.

Correction—where we'd been taken to.

I squeezed the girl's hand. We hadn't let go of each other since the moment I prayed against her ear. For hours, we'd secretly held hands. Whatever comfort she was able to draw from me rejuvenated my need for survival. I had a reason now to be strong, to live, for this young girl and her twin brother.

Doors slammed outside of the trailer, chatter ensued, less urgent than when we were loaded up from the house, but still an edgy, uncomfortable excitement. And still in Spanish, I noted.

The locks were lifted, the door opened.

To my surprise, it was still night, but instead of briny sea-salt air, a potent scent of earth, dirt, and lush plant life swept into the cab. I inhaled deeply, reminded of a tropical candle my mother would burn in the summertime.

Guns were pointed at our faces. We were ordered to stand.

My knees shook as I pulled myself up from the floor. I helped the children up, using every ounce of energy I had in me.

We were marched out of the truck, eyes down, guns at our temples. I stayed close behind the girl so the guards wouldn't see the bloodstains on her shorts.

The ground was warm and moist beneath my bare feet. The scent of fresh, dewy vegetation was even stronger the farther we walked, but it was the noise that captured my attention. Despite being nighttime, birds chirped among a steady buzz of insects, a deafening white noise. Frogs croaked in tune with screaming insects. Life—the area was teeming with it.

I chanced a peek. A dense forest surrounded us, barely visible in the blackness, but a looming presence nonetheless.

We were in the middle of the jungle.

We were marched up a steep, narrow dirt road. Sharp rocks cut into the bottom of my feet, but I didn't care. I was too busy inhaling the clean air, listening to the rustle of leaves, feeling the breeze against my skin. Still hot and humid, but clean, devoid of exhaust, smoke, and pollution.

Soon I realized that it wasn't a road we were hiking, but a driveway that ended at the top of the hill. Ahead stood a large log cabin surrounded by trees. At each peak of the sprawling structure, blinding post lights shone into the woods, reminding me of a prison.

It was then that I realized how silent we all were. Not

only the slaves, but the guards. No one was speaking. There was a nervous energy bouncing between us all.

Why?

I focused on my feet, one after the other, chancing peeks the farther up the drive we were led.

The building wasn't so much a cabin, I realized, as a lodge. An old, abandoned vacation destination, perhaps. Vacant for a long time, based on the rotted wood planks, and the green vines that grew up the sides, stretching all the way to the dilapidated roof.

It was probably beautiful at one time. Luxurious, even.

We were marched onto a massive porch, then into the lodge and onto cool hardwood floors, stained and scuffed. The room smelled musty, of mildew and dirt, this confirming that it had been vacant for a very long time.

Orders were shouted, echoing down long, vacant halls.

I thought of Ardri, the King, and wondered if he were there. Secretly hoping he was, and then berating myself for how ridiculous that was.

The guards guided us down a long corridor. I heard the *thump, thump, thump* of footsteps descending a staircase before I saw it.

Another damn basement.

At the bottom was an endless concrete floor lined with dozens of tall dog cages, much like the ones in the house before, each with a number attached to the door. The space was massive, and I could see at least four long hopper windows, opened to allow for fresh air.

Apparently, this was our new home—but not new to some.

Half the cages were already occupied with slaves, mostly women, but also young girls and one teenage boy. They seemed worse off than we were, skinnier, paler, more sickly.

Long stringy hair and malnourished bony bodies made them resemble the faceless zombies I'd imagined in the other house. While our eyes reflected fear, their eyes were hard, a venomous hatred beaming at us from the red rims.

I was shoved into the cage numbered 647. The cage door slammed behind me, echoing the closing of the others.

Locks were slid into place. The lights were turned out.

We were left alone.

There were no cries that night . . . which was somehow more unnerving.

12

ROMAN

"How much longer?" I asked the driver as the Jeep Wrangler jolted over the muddy dirt road.

"About thirty-five more minutes, *señor*."

Staring out the window from where I sat in the back seat, I forced patience. I was eager, anxious. Ready.

And hot as fuck.

Slanted beams of sunlight cut through the jungle canopy like swords of fire. Long black shadows stretched across the narrow one-way road ahead of us. Trees formed a tunnel overhead, the thick shade doing little to shield us from the sweltering tropical humidity.

"Turn up the air," I said, yanking at the collar of my suit.

Fucking suits.

Lucas Ruiz's gaze flicked to me in the rearview mirror before he clicked down the temperature, and I noticed a sheen of sweat on his forehead, among a few other things.

His skin was darker than when I'd last seen him, and I wondered if he'd taken some time off, perhaps a beach vacation. His pitch-black hair was damp and mussed from repeatedly running his fingers through it. His uniform, dark army fatigues, clung tightly to his muscular body, the fabric damp with sweat.

I wasn't the only one anxious.

I glanced at my watch—

TIME: 7:04 P.M.
TEMPERATURE: 97°
HUMIDITY: 87%

It should have added:

FEELS-LIKE TEMPERATURE: WADING THROUGH A RIVER OF MUD.

We hadn't passed a single vehicle, ATV, or hiker since passing a sign that read:

HOMBRE MUERTO TRAIL
— CAUTION —

There are no places to obtain supplies or get help until Diablo Bridge 87 miles north. Do not attempt this section unless you have a minimum of ten days of supplies and are fully equipped, as the difficulty of this trail should not be underestimated. This trail contains wild animals that are unpredictable and aggressive. Visitors walking this trail do so at their own risk.

Yes, we were literally out in the middle of nowhere in the

Sierra Madre Mountains, one of the world's largest mountain ranges, spanning from northern Mexico to Guatemala.

Considered the wildest, most untamed section of the Sierra Madre Mountains, the Sierra Madre Occidental was a famous destination for hikers and thrill seekers alike. Most popular was the trail named *Hombre Muerto*, which translated to Dead Man's Trail, that led to a section of mountains so vast and breathtaking, they were often compared to the Grand Canyon. Portions of the Sierra Madre Occidental were known for their extensive network of caves, hundreds hidden between rocks, behind thick vegetation, this being my favorite feature of the mountain range.

Dead Man's Trail snaked through the densest and most remote section of the mountains, with no easy access to civilization for almost a hundred miles. It took most hikers eight days to hike from one end to the other, assuming they made it.

Marked by soaring peaks, steep valleys, treacherous canyons, plunging waterfalls, and rushing rivers, the terrain was infamous for challenging even the most experienced outdoorsmen. Considered one of Mexico's most unforgiving terrains, the most common cause of death ranged from heart attacks to drownings to falling from cliffs.

Fauna includes bats, lizards, snakes, black bears, mountain lions, bobcats, and the ever-elusive jaguar. Wolves were rarer to see, but no less deadly. Over three hundred bird species called the jungle home, many of which were endangered, such as the thick-billed parrot and the colorful military macaw.

The most fearsome and brutal inhabitants of the area were, however, the insects that ruled the jungle. Venomous spiders, giant centipedes, and the dreaded bullet ant, whose bite triggers excruciating and debilitating pain for twenty-four hours. This, however, was nothing compared to the infestation of black flies and mosquitos that feasted on every inch of exposed skin, no matter day or night.

Though, the locals will tell you the wild animals and blood-sucking insects are nothing compared to the spirits that lurk in the shadows. Dead Man's Trail is infamous for its disappearances, unsolved murders, and multiple reported hauntings.

In 2009, American tourist Emily Parker was kidnapped from the trail and held captive for three days in a tent before being bludgeoned to death by a car jack. In 2001, Louise Morales and her sister Maria went missing from the trail, their decapitated bodies later found on Christmas Day. Dozens of children, families, and even park rangers have gone missing in this area of the jungle, their bodies yet to be discovered.

Hikers being tracked by faceless figures, campers awaking to eyeless ghosts watching from the mist, whispers on the wind, strange lights and orbs flickering through the trees, are only a few of the urban legends that haunt Dead Man's Trail.

Little do the well-meaning gossips know, these stories didn't compare to the real horror hidden in these woods. One that I was about to face head-on.

I smashed a bug against the window, then flicked its carcass to the floorboard. "Let's recap."

The Jeep hit another bottomless pit in the road, jostling the cab and sending maps and papers tumbling to the floorboard.

Lucas regained control. "Last known communication was two days ago, between him and a high-ranking official I spoke with. Conor is on his way here, to the lodge."

"And you're sure he was here two weeks ago?"

"Yes. I didn't see him personally, but that is what I understand." Lucas spoke perfect English, only a hint of his Spanish accent sneaking through. "Had a business meeting or something. Stayed for five days, shored up a few things, assessed his inventory—"

"Inventory, meaning slaves."

"Yes."

"How much time did he spend with Samantha, one on one?"

Lucas shook his head. "I don't know. Like I said, I didn't see him."

I frowned, turning to the window.

"Anyway, his current location is unknown."

"He was in Thailand," I said.

Lucas frowned, glancing in the rearview mirror.

"Conor was in Thailand for four days until he boarded a plane yesterday."

"How do you know this?" Lucas asked.

"My sources. His plane lands at Licenciado Gustavo International in exactly seventeen minutes."

"What was he doing in Thailand?"

"Selling children."

Lucas shifted in his seat, a line of disapproval creasing his forehead. And he didn't know the half of it.

Conor Cussane had recently expanded his operations into the child-harvesting sector, joining forces with a trafficking network in Thailand, home to one of the largest baby factories in the world. There, young women are kidnapped, raped, and impregnated. They're held in horrific conditions until their babies are born, only for the babies to be ripped from their mother's arms the moment they are cleaned, and sold for no more than two thousand US dollars.

Two thousand dollars.

"I'd like to know who your sources are that disclosed this information," Lucas said.

"I'm sure you would."

My friend and undercover agent with the Mexican intelligence agency, the CNI, looked in the rearview mirror. He paused a moment as if choosing his next words carefully. "We've been working together for how long now?"

The question was rhetorical because neither of us could remember. Five years? Ten? Despite that, we both held secrets from each other. We knew it and respected it. It was part of the work we did.

But something about this mission was different. The stakes were high—for both of us.

"How is the lodge?" I asked, diverting Lucas away from his curiosity about my sources. Hell, I didn't even know their real names—and they sure as hell didn't know mine.

"Let's just say I hope you got a good deal on it."

"Are you staying there?" I asked.

"There, in my car, wherever. I can't be inside all the time —the fucking noise, man. The drugs . . . it's constant."

I nodded, understanding the wear of being undercover twenty-four hours a day. The vital need for a few moments of solace, a respite from the ungodly world we chose to enter.

"When this is done, I'm gone," Lucas said. "Back home for some time off. I leave in two days, which means that's how long you have my help here. You're on your own after that."

I sat up, pinning him in the rearview mirror. "The transport isn't supposed to happen for *six* more days, Lucas."

"Conor will be here by then, which means I will no longer exist to you, anyway."

"Not unless I need you."

This time, he pinned me. "My daughter is due to have a baby within the week. I'm leaving, Roman."

I inhaled. After a moment, I nodded. "Understood."

"Is your company on the ready if you need them?"

"No."

His brows raised. "Do they know you're here now?"

"No."

Truth was, not a single person at Astor Stone, Inc. knew where I was or what I was doing. Neither my boss, nor my teammates.

After Samantha had been declared dead, I was expected back at the office. My decision to go rogue on the case was an act of rebellion that would not only get me fired, but probably killed, by the hands of Astor himself.

No one disobeyed Astor Stone. Only me, when my entire life had built to this moment.

Lucas shook his head but bit his tongue.

"How are the operations at the lodge?" I asked.

"The lodge is a shitshow. The men are nervous; everything has to be perfect. For most of them, it's their first time to meet Conor. Very big deal for them. And you, for that matter. They are always nervous around you."

"How many guards total?"

"Four as of last night. They take shifts guarding the house. Two on at a time, while the others go into town for food or whatever. Then they switch."

"Did you see her?"

"Your American? Samantha?"

"Yes," I hissed between clenched teeth. Something about hearing her name on his lips . . .

"Yes, I've seen her."

"What condition is she in now?"

"Since you saw her yesterday?"

"Yes."

"Well, she's alive."

"Define alive, Lucas."

"She's in decent shape."

"Define decent."

"As you know, Conor has demanded that she be kept in clean shape. Unharmed, unmarred."

"Aside from losing her finger," I snapped.

Lucas was silent for a moment, and I made a mental note to rein in the ridiculous emotions this girl ignited in me.

"It's all part of it," he said eventually. "She will be branded soon, you know. They are all to be branded before they get shipped out."

I closed my eyes, forcing my jaw to relax.

It doesn't matter, I reminded myself. *Conor is the main target. Conor, Conor . . .*

"How many slaves are there total?" I asked.

"Sixteen."

Blinking, I stilled. "That's four more than you originally told me, Lucas."

"We made some stops on the way."

"Stops that you failed to communicate."

"They were unplanned."

"That's no excuse. How many and where?"

"Two stops. A few refugees and an American tourist."

Fucking Christ.

"Have you confirmed the sale?"

"Yes. As you know, the transport is scheduled for six days from today. The girls will be loaded up in the same van they arrived in last night and taken to a dock in Tampico. About a fifteen-hour drive."

"How is Conor planning to get past Port Authority?"

Lucas lifted his hand from the steering wheel and rubbed the tips of his fingers together.

Money. Conor paid someone off to look the other way.

"From there," he said, "they'll board a fishing boat, then be taken to a cargo ship that will take them the rest of the way."

To the Gauteng Province in South Africa, he meant, one of the largest, most savage human-trafficking markets in the world. There, humans are sold to the most immoral vile traffickers, who sell the women to sweatshops to work twenty hours a day under inhumane conditions, to baby farms where they're raped and impregnated repeatably, or to twisted doctors where they're murdered, their organs sold on the black market.

If Samantha Greene thought her captivity was hard now, it was about to get much worse—if I didn't get her out in time, while somehow keeping my cover.

"There are two auctions Conor is planning to attend once there." Lucas swatted a fly from his face. "The slaves will be split between the two. One caters to a much more sophisticated crowd."

I snorted. "You mean politicians and businessmen?"

"Something like that."

"What are his plans for Samantha specifically?"

"As I understand it, she will go and be trained and bedded by Conor himself, will be taken with him wherever he goes once there. Once she has supplied him adequate offspring, she will be sold. She will go for a very high price, considering her connection to Conor. White women are sold the quickest too. Also, she's beautiful."

A sharp pain scissored through my gut.

"Why did he choose her, specifically? Do you know?"

"She's beautiful. Not much deeper than that. She's young, *and* Conor has a thing for American women."

I contemplated the pros and cons of being blessed with beauty. In America, women pay thousands of dollars to enhance their appearance, as this is valued almost as much as health. However, in most third world countries, women hide their beauty from the evil men who live among them, and some even consider it a curse.

The day Samantha was taken, the day her picture was sent to Conor to add to his files as one of his new slaves, her beauty was her curse.

Lucas hit the brakes, easing over a large rock in the road. "I guess you realize what a huge deal it is that Conor is willing to meet you."

"He doesn't want to meet me, Lucas; he wants to work with me. I have ties to both the Irish and US markets. Of course he wants to work with me."

"You also have a bottomless bank account."

Money. It was always about money. The entire world revolved around money.

Lucas slowed around another hairpin corner, this one half obstructed by a fallen tree.

Checking my GPS, I said, "Pull over."

"Wh— Here?"

"Yes, pull over."

Lucas steered off the dirt road, pulling next to a thriving fern bush, its massive leaves dwarfing the Jeep.

I glanced at my wristwatch.

For a time, we sat in silence.

One minute became ten, then twenty. Finally . . .

"Jesus *Christ*."

A man dressed in full army fatigues fought his way through the brush, the blade of a K-Bar gripped between his teeth, a massive pack on his back, a gun in each hand. Face paint covered every inch of his skin.

I grinned, opening the door.

13

ROMAN

*T*he six-foot-three special ops Marine stopped on a dime the moment I unfolded myself from the Jeep.

Scowling down at my suit and shiny wingtips, he said, "Oh, fuck *you*," in a thick Southern accent.

We shook hands.

"Bear, you look like shit."

"And you look like you just walked off the set of *Miami Vice*. What the hell is this shit?" He flicked the collar of my suit. "Who is this? Jorge Armani?"

"It's Giorgio, you half-baked hillbilly."

"This coming from a guy who grew up in the dumpsters of Dublin." Bear inspected Lucas, still seated behind the steering wheel, trying to figure out what the hell was going on. "I thought it was supposed to be just us."

"That's Lucas Ruiz, with the Mexican CNI."

"Mexican intelligence agency?"

"Yes."

"He's undercover too?"

"Yes, for over a decade."

Bear dipped his chin in approval. Despite the scarce details I'd provided him when calling in a favor by requesting his assistance in an "off-the-books" op, Bear trusted me, as I did him—with my life.

Josh Ellis, known as Bear, wasn't only the kind of scrappy, ruthless guy you wanted on your side during a bar fight, but the kind who would give you the shirt off his back. Born and bred in the South, Bear had walked away from his family, his Texas mansion, and a hefty inheritance to join the Marines after 9/11. The forty-one-year-old Texas native was as good as gold in my book, and there was no one else I'd ask to help me on this mission.

"Good to see you, man." Our gazes locked for a second with the respect and loyalty bred between brothers who had shed blood together in Afghanistan. "Now, get in."

"My fucking pleasure."

Bear lumbered around the Jeep and collapsed into the back, exhausted from a multi-day hike through the woods, which he'd deemed necessary to avoid being seen or tracked. In my message days earlier, I'd provided Bear with nothing but a short summary of what I needed from him, a date and time, and the GPS coordinates for the meeting place.

I knew he'd be there.

After taking a quick glance over my shoulder, I also slid into the back seat and made introductions.

"What's with the face paint?" I asked Bear as Lucas lurched the Jeep back onto the trail.

"It's not paint. It's dirt and deer shit."

"Jesus." I screwed my face in disgust when the smell hit me. "You roll around in it, or what?"

"Rubbed it on my skin after I ran out of DEET a few

miles back." His eyes were wide with wonder. "I've never seen mosquitos this big in my life, man."

"I've got a few more cans of bug spray in the back," Lucas said, "and some netting."

"I'll take it all." Bear unearthed a water bottle from his pack. After chugging half, he wiped his chin. "So, what's the plan?"

I pulled a pack from the floorboard and tossed it to him. "We're going to drop you off a mile from where we're staying. You'll hike northwest for three and a half klicks to a cliff with spotty views of the lodge. Set up shop there and wait for orders."

"Want me to deploy a drone?"

"No," Lucas said from the front. "Too risky. The men are too anxious. They'll spot it."

"Why so anxious?" Bear unzipped the pack I'd just tossed him and began sifting through the contents, which included one week's worth of MREs, water and water purification tablets, bedding, clothing, SAT communication equipment, first aid kit, ammo, fire-starting kit, flashlights, bug spray, a fifth of Jack, and a box of condoms—a joke between us, and I'll leave it at that.

He unzipped the side pocket and lifted the grenade buried inside. Grinning at me, he said, "A bulldozer?"

"Did you expect anything less?"

"Not from you, man." Bear dipped his chin in thanks, then tucked the deadly explosive device safely back into the pocket. "So, what are the bastards anxious about?"

"One, Ardri here in the back seat." Lucas gestured to me in the back.

"Ardri?" Bear asked, laughing.

"It means *high king* in Gaelic, a moniker your boy earned over the years."

Bear looked at me. "You've become quite the big deal in the human-trafficking circle?"

Lucas nodded from the front seat. "Ardri is notorious. The men fear him just as much as they admire him. He has lots of money—pays big bucks for the women. And he always, *always* wears a suit."

"Your mama must be so proud," Bear said with a tsk-tsk.

Lucas glanced in the rearview mirror at us. "More than him, though, they're nervous about meeting the leader of the Cussane Network."

I nodded. "The guards see it as a huge opportunity to move into Conor Cussane's circle if they can impress him."

"I'd like to move the barrel of my shotgun into his circle."

Lucas scowled from the front seat, and Bear grinned.

"Anyway," I said, "I've got six days to get the American tourist out before she's shipped overseas."

"I don't understand. Why you can't just buy her now? You're in this Conor guy's inner circle, right? Can't you just—"

"Yes, but we've never met face-to-face."

Until now.

Bear shrugged. "Okay, well, whatever. Just buy her, and let's get the hell out of this sweltering hellhole."

"You don't get it," I said. "Conor owns her personally. He's claimed her as *his*, not part of the network."

"So he won't sell her to you?"

"Didn't say that."

"You kind of just did say exactly that."

I shrugged. "I'm going to offer more than she's worth."

Bear lifted a brow. "You just said a mouthful there, bro."

I stilled a moment, considering the verbiage I'd used and how disgusting it was.

Embarrassed, I cleared my throat. "I'm going to get her alone before Conor gets there, and get as many details about the time she's spent with him as I can so I'm not going in blind."

"You think he told her where he keeps his USB?"

"Intel suggests he keeps it on him at all times, and if she's been with him, yeah. Maybe it's simply in his wallet. I need to know if she's seen it. Then, after he arrives, I'll make the offer to Conor directly for her."

"What makes you sure he'll accept your offer?"

"Conor lives for money. I'll make it worth it to him."

"How much are we talking about here?"

My entire worth, I thought.

"Why not just save your money and steal her in the middle of the night," Bear asked, "and be done with it?"

I shook my head. "Everyone is expecting me. It's my lodge they're staying in."

And also, Bear didn't know the details of my full plan.

A hint of nerves jolted me.

This was it. My once-in-a-lifetime moment. No second chances.

Bear grunted. "What time is this Conor guy coming?"

"Soon. You've got the plane at the airport on standby?"

"Yes, as you requested."

"Good. When I hand her off to you, take her exactly where I instructed in my email."

"Assuming that everything goes off without a hitch, right? That you buy this missing girl from one of the most ruthless human traffickers on the planet, and then just walk right out the door with her, lickety-split."

"It'll go off without a hitch," I said confidently. It had to. There was no other option.

"And then you'll just head back to the airport, call it a

day, collect your check from the government, and go find a bar somewhere and drink yourself to sleep?"

"Something like that."

Bear glanced at Lucas before looking back at me. He lowered his voice. "I don't like it."

"I don't care."

"How many men are coming with this Conor guy?" Bear asked.

"According to Lucas, four armed guards are at the lodge now."

"I didn't ask how many men were at the lodge. I asked how many men Conor is bringing with him—in *addition* to these four armed guards."

Truth was, I didn't know. More than Lucas and I could handle if shit went sideways.

Reading my non-answer as answer enough, Bear blew out a long breath and sat back. After a minute, a smirk tugged at the corner of his mouth. "Good to be working with you again, bud."

I dipped my chin, guilt twisting my stomach.

14

$\mathcal{W}$e were given food, water, and matching dog collars with tags. Mine read 647. I wondered if that were how many slaves had been held captive at the hands of this evil group.

We were provided baby wipes to bathe, toothpaste but no brush, and kept in our respective dog cages, aside from monitored short bathroom breaks.

I didn't know where the children were. They had been separated while being marched out of the truck the night before.

I was surrounded by new faces, new slaves. New moans, cries, incoherent mumbling. Dead eyes.

I was pretending to sleep when the basement door opened. Instinctively, I hugged my knees to my chest, making myself appear as small and insignificant as possible. Not far from how I actually felt, come to think of it.

I listened to the footsteps descend into the room. The low hushed voices in Spanish once again. Whoever was with the guards appeared to be viewing each of the slaves, pausing at each cage as the guards relayed details of "the product."

My heart started to pound. Were we being shown like cattle at the fair? Was someone about to buy us? Were we to be traded?

The footsteps drew closer, and a breeze from the opened door swept past.

My eyes shot open. I recognized the fresh, citrus scent.

The King.

I squeezed my eyes shut again, but this time peeked through the slits. A familiar pair of shiny black wingtips appeared in front of my cage, next to two sets of scuffed combat boots.

Ardri, I heard from one of the men.

My pulse kickstarted. He was back, the man who had visited the other location. The man I couldn't stop thinking about.

After Capitán provided my specs to the King, there was a long pause of silence. I could feel their eyes on me. Somehow, I knew a decision was being contemplated. I waited on bated breath for the King to speak.

Finally, he did, three little words that changed the course of my life from that day forward. "Give me her."

The guards stilled, hesitating.

"I said," the King repeated, his voice low and menacing. "Give me her."

One of the men said something in Spanish. He spoke timidly, and I caught the name Conor Cussane.

The King reached into his pocket, and without a word, began doling out stacks of Mexican money to the men.

The guards snatched the paper like starving children, stuffing them into their pockets.

"Five minutes," the King said, then turned on his heel and disappeared upstairs.

15

SAM

I was removed from my cage and, with a rifle to my head, taken upstairs, retracing the same path I'd marched the day before. My hands remained cuffed in front of my body.

While keeping my head down, I took in as much as I could.

The lights were on, which meant it was dark outside. Nighttime. The smell of a microwave dinner lingered in the air, mixing with the pungent scent of pot. A TV or a radio droned on somewhere in the distance. The evening news, I noticed, and tried desperately to make out the words in the hope of learning my exact location. No luck.

I was guided down a dimly lit long, wide corridor. Walls of windows lined the sides, black with night. A full moon hung low in the sky, washing a silver glow over endless tree-tops. Dust bunnies coated the trim along the floor, and piles of trash had gathered in the corners.

The corridor split. The barrel of the gun tapped the side of my head, indicating that I turn right.

I was forced into a small room with a bed. A wooden rocking chair sat next to a closed window. A few boxes lay haphazardly on the hardwood floor. A lamp was on in the corner, casting a dim gold light over the room. The strong, powdery scent of fabric softener saturated the air, suggesting the sheets and comforter had been recently washed.

A video camera was erected on a tripod in the corner.

At the sight of it, my stomach rolled. Was I going to be filmed?

The guards stripped me of my housedress, their disgusting bloodshot eyes raking over my naked body. My hands were uncuffed. My right wrist was secured to the bedpost with a long chain—just enough slack to allow for movement on the bed, I noticed, but definitely not long enough to reach the window. Then I was left alone, staring at the door.

Paralyzed by fear, I stood there naked in the deafening silence. Seconds slowly ticked by, then minutes. Eventually, I sat on the edge of the bed, perching like a little bird. Waiting, waiting, waiting.

For what?

I stared at the closed door.

For what?

After what seemed like hours, the silence was broken by the sound of footsteps approaching in the hallway. I surged to my feet like a soldier, my heart leaping into my throat.

The door opened.

The King entered in all his dashingly dangerous glory. Two guards hovered behind him.

My heart stuttered as our eyes locked.

He looked different in the light of the lamp, impossibly

handsome. He was wearing a flawless navy suit that appeared to be tailored to his body, emphasizing his broad shoulders, small waist, and thick thighs. The white dress shirt he wore underneath was starched to perfection, the dark tie simple, yet elegant, the silk fabric undoubtedly costing as much as the black wingtips.

He looked like a million dollars.

I looked like street trash.

My pulse began to race wildly.

The King closed the door in the guards' faces, but they didn't leave. Instead, the horny bastards gathered on the other side, listening, whispering, peeking through the cracks, awaiting their entertainment for the evening.

And what entertainment was I to provide them?

Remembering the rules, I quickly looked down at the floor. I felt myself go rigid, the chain around my wrist clanking against the bedpost as my body stiffened with insecurity.

I was ashamed. Not just because I was naked and chained to a bed, but because of the bruises, the weight I'd lost, the scars, the pastiness of my skin. The dry flecks of dead flesh. My unshaved legs, armpits, privates.

My cheeks burned.

I don't look like this, I wanted to scream to him. *I don't look like this!*

I'm beautiful. In real life, I'm beautiful.

I am not *a slave.*

To my utter shock, I felt a rush of emotions, accompanied by the sting of tears. I quickly forced them away, attributing this reaction to the man before me. The other men didn't make me insecure, they made me savage.

What was it about him—*the King?*

He slowly crossed the room, the click of his steps slow compared to the wild beating of my heart. I could feel his eyes like green fire on my face as he turned off the camera and closed the window shade.

Tap, tap, tap.

I forced myself not to flinch as the King closed the few feet between us, stopping inches in front of my trembling naked body.

I felt so small in front of him. His body, his presence towered over me. *A man*—a real, intimidating, powerful *man*.

My pulse roared in my ears as I awaited what would happen next.

Finally, he spoke. "Let me see."

Goose bumps raced over my arms, my body viscerally responding to the deep voice with the Irish lilt.

I swallowed past the knot in my throat. "See what?" I whispered, keeping my face downcast.

"Your hand."

Shocked, I looked up. Electric-green eyes stared down at me, as cold as ice, his square jaw locked. I hesitated.

"Let me see," he said again.

Slowly, I lifted my unchained hand and turned over my palm. When he took it, a zing of electricity sparked at the touch. Humiliated, I closed my eyes and inhaled as he examined the stitches that ran along the nub where my pinky finger had once been.

I was so *embarrassed.*

I stared down at his perfect fancy shoes as he stared down at me. He was studying me. I felt like I was being assessed, judged like cattle.

Seconds ticked by. Anger and frustration began to simmer on top of the humiliation.

What an asshole.

Anger erupted, and I jerked back my hand. Glaring at him, I pulled my shoulders back and stood tall, displaying my naked body unabashedly.

"Just get it over with already," I said, seething. "Just get it fucking done."

16

*S*amantha's words hit me like a tidal wave as I met those slitted hazel eyes glaring into mine.

The bite to the words, the abhorrence. The *strength*.

Her body trembled. Not with fear, but with anger. With that God-given grit that all of us possess but only a few understand how to properly unleash.

Samantha Greene wasn't scared of me. Or if she was, she was forcing herself to be strong, gripping onto her one remaining shred of self-respect with bloody fingernails.

The woman still had fight in her. Despite everything she'd been through, Samantha Greene refused to give up on *herself*.

And I respected the hell out of it.

A flurry of something that resembled emotions spun inside me. A mixture of gut-wrenching sorrow at the survival mode she'd adopted—*had* to adopt. Samantha assumed she was about to be raped, but because she knew that fighting was useless, she'd learned that she had to accept certain things, and Jesus Christ, the woman did it with fucking dignity.

I studied her, experiencing a mad rush of anger that she'd been forced into this situation, fury at the men responsible for it, and a deep-rooted understanding of the vile hatred she had for me in that moment. But most of all, I felt complete shock at the strength and vehemence, the backbone on this small, vulnerable woman standing in front of me.

"Get it over with already."

I was flummoxed at how wrong I'd been in my original assessment of her. During my research, I'd labeled Samantha Greene as an extremely emotional, mentally fragile train wreck. As nothing special. A kid.

The woman was anything but.

Rarely am I surprised. I take pride in my ability to accurately assess and read someone with little to no information. Nothing forces you to become an expert at sizing up people like a childhood spent living on the streets. Whether by choice or survival, I'd developed a keen intuition before the age of ten.

It failed me with this woman.

My heart pounded, and I didn't fully understand why. Why was she having such an effect on me? Samantha Greene wasn't the first woman I'd seen chained and naked, not the first woman I'd been attracted to. Nor the first I'd had to pretend to bed while undercover.

An anger I hadn't felt before simmered in my stomach. Samantha Greene was so small and innocent. She was a teacher, for Christ's sake.

What had she been subjected to?

What was I too late to save her from?

What did she think of me? That I was a nasty old man? That I was evil?

And how far was that from the truth?

A sudden urge overcame me to make her to think other-wise. To prove to her I wasn't the vile person she thought I was.

In that moment, the tables turned. Everything became about *her*. Saving Samantha became equally as important as destroying Conor Cussane.

But how? I had to stick to the plan.

I never deviated from a plan. Not *ever*.

We stared at each other, the electricity between us so strong, it blurred everything else around us.

I wanted to soothe her, sweep her up in my arms and tell her everything was going to be okay. That I was going to ensure that.

But I couldn't.

This isn't the fucking plan.

I had to find another way to get her alone without the goons waiting outside. To ask her about the USB. To replace my fucking spine that she seemed to have obliterated with a single flutter of her eyelashes.

I had to wait for Conor to arrive to execute the plan I'd spent days outlining. I had to meet him. After all, I'd worked my entire life for this moment.

This isn't the fucking plan, Roman.

Staring down at her, I thought of the guards on the other side of the door. And suddenly, this moment became a test for us both.

17

"*G*et on the bed." The King's eyes narrowed, his voice low and menacing, the spark I'd seen seconds earlier suddenly replaced by darkness.

My stomach dropped to my feet.

"I said, get on the bed."

Keeping my gaze on his, I slowly lowered myself to a seated position on the edge of the bed. The chain that bound my wrist clinked against the headboard.

"*On* the bed," he said.

I glanced at the door, where I could practically hear the guards breathing, then back at him.

Slowly, I scooted farther onto the bed, lifted one leg onto the mattress, then the next, demanding his eyes to remain on mine while my naked legs momentarily spread.

His gaze never once wavered.

The King loosened his tie and began to unbutton the collar of his shirt. "Lay down."

Stiffly, I lowered onto my back, but his eyes remained on mine. Never once did they trail down my body. Not a single time.

The King slipped out of his suit jacket and tossed it on the bed, the collar catching my bare foot, sending a shot of electricity up my leg.

I smelled him again, inhaling deeply as if his scent were a drug I couldn't get enough of.

As he pulled his dress shirt loose from his pants, our eyes remained locked. He unbuttoned the top button, then another, then another.

My breathing became heavy, my skin hot. I fought to keep my eyes on his while taking in the blurred area just out of focus. A tanned chest and rippled abs.

A tingling pulse fired up between my legs.

My reaction to this man was jarring. I felt myself get wet, ready. How could that be, especially under such horrific circumstances? I wasn't even sure if I'd ever feel desire for a man again.

I waited with bated breath for his next command, my chest rising and falling quickly with adrenaline, his breathing calm and controlled. Confident. *Sexy as fuck.*

The fingers of my unchained hand slowly fisted the comforter below my body.

He licked his lips.

I lifted my knees, spread my legs.

The vein running down the side of his neck began throbbing. A sheen of sweat shimmered on his forehead. The cool, calm demeanor was cracking.

I spread open my legs, my sex throbbing with desire.

We stared at each other, the sound of my heartbeat in my ears absolutely deafening.

Then, without a word, the King turned around and walked out of the room, his shirt open and his jacket on the bed.

I jumped as the door slammed behind him.

Freezing in place, I snapped my legs shut, wondering what *the hell* just happened.

18

*H*ours passed. Outside the window, the moon slowly rose.

I was still handcuffed and chained to the bed naked—well, semi-naked, I should say. I'd draped the suit jacket the King had left over my shoulders, threading my unchained arm through one of the sleeves.

The smell was *him*, the soft buttery fabric was *him*.

The comfort was *him*.

I couldn't help but wonder if he'd left the jacket on purpose.

The night was relatively quiet after the King had left me. A few screams and howls came from the basement below, eventually fading to silence as I assumed the slaves fell asleep. Based on the position of the moon, it was midnight, possibly early morning.

The guards had begun their usual evening of debauchery, drinking, smoking, doing whatever drugs were available. The heavy thud of bass echoed somewhere down the hall, the mind-numbing pounding punctuated by occasional drunken laughter.

I searched for *his* voice, *his* laugh, but there was nothing.

Where was he? Where did he go?

Was he with the guards? Indulging? Laughing? Tormenting women? Was he evil like them?

Why hadn't he returned?

I hated myself for how long I'd contemplated that last question. The screwed-up part of it was that I blamed myself. I'd convinced myself that I—my face, my body, my manners—weren't good enough for him. That's why he hadn't returned. I wasn't desirable enough, attractive enough. He'd probably gone on to find another slave, to spend the evening with her.

I'd fucking spread my legs for the man, open and willing —wet, for Christ's sake—and yet I still wasn't good enough for the King. There were slaves better than me.

I needed to be better at my job.

It was the mindfuck of all mindfucks. The kind of thought process that the world of human trafficking made you think was normal. Truly, I was becoming brainwashed.

I was changing. I could feel it in my bones, my soul. This life was beginning to change who I was at my core, and I *hated* it.

My attention was pulled to footsteps coming down the hall, and my heart skipped a beat. I pushed off the bed and stood tall and strong, my shoulders back.

The brass doorknob turned, the door opened, and two guards stumbled into the room, stinking drunk, their eyes ablaze with drugs and lust.

My stomach dropped to my feet, the instant shot of panic ripping my breath away.

One of them closed the door and locked it behind him.

No.

No, no, no.

Their beady black eyes locked on mine as they crossed the room, licking their lips like dogs. One was no more than twenty years old, eighteen maybe, wearing a pair of baggy jeans with holes and a black T-shirt. The other, at least fifty, was dressed in army fatigues.

They spoke quietly to each other in Spanish, wicked grins cracking their dirty, acne-scarred faces. They were here in secret. The King didn't know. And they were up to no good.

No, no, no.

The older guard spat on me.

I forced my eyes to stay open, my demeanor stoic while I felt the disgusting slime slide down my cheek.

Do not let them see you cry.

The men stripped me of the King's jacket and pushed me onto the bed. The older man spat obscenities at me while the teenager laughed. I got the sense the man was training him. How to be an evil rapist, how to fit in among the worst humanity had to offer.

They unzipped their pants, stumbling and grabbing onto each other for support while muttering snide remarks back and forth. The smell of sour liquor filled the air.

My legs were thrust open, my muscles screaming in protest. They sniffed dramatically, taking in my scent like dogs.

Tears welled in my eyes, a mixture of both fear and hate roaring through my veins.

I could smell their privates as they unfolded their erections from their pants and crawled onto the bed. I was flipped onto my stomach, my cuffed wrist painfully twisted.

My entire body began to shake with fear.

There was laughter, then fingers on my flesh. I squeezed my eyes shut, buried my face into the comforter.

Somewhere over the rainbow . . .

Nails raked down my back.

Bluebirds fly . . .

My buttocks were spread open.

And the dream that you dare to . . .

Suddenly, a loud boom shook the room. The door burst open, the knob clattering to the floor after it slammed against the wall.

The older man was lifted from my back and thrown into the wall.

I screamed and flipped over, the rub of the metal cuff burning my wrist.

The teenager jumped off the bed, ready to fight, but was immediately silenced by a blow to his face. Blood splattered the wall, and what I assumed was teeth ticked onto the floor.

The King moved like water as he fought off both men with lightning-fast strikes and calculated blows. He moved with the ease and smoothness of someone who had been expertly trained in lethal combat. Like an animal, leading a deadly dance of speed and strength.

I heard the sickening pop of bone, then another. The teenager fell to the floor, his neck obviously broken.

The King wrestled the older man onto the floor and wrapped his hands around his throat. His white dress shirt was covered in blood spatters, like someone had flung a red paintbrush at him.

"Conor . . ." The man gasped for breath.

The King slammed the man's head against the floor.

"Conor, no . . ."

The King stilled, the man's words penetrating the haze of rage. He frowned.

The man struggled, writhing in pain in the King's grasp. "Please, Conor . . ."

I watched the King's face twist in confusion.

"Conor, please, don't kill me. I have been loyal to you, to the—"

"What the fuck?" the King snapped, banging the man's head once more. "I'm not Conor, you sick fuck."

"Conor . . ." The man's voice cracked. "Please . . . everyone knows . . . I won't tell . . ."

"Everyone knows what?"

"That you're him. You are Conor Cussane. P—plea—"

The man's jaw went slack and his eyes glazed over as he took his last breath.

19

*M*y chest heaved as I stared at the carnage on the floor, at the man who had just saved my life.

The King's hands were frozen around the dead man's neck, his brow furrowed with confusion, his skin speckled with blood. Noise sounded down the hall, but the King didn't notice, still staring at the man's face.

"Conor." I hissed his name quietly.

His intensity startled me. Was this man friend or foe? Good or bad?

Looking up at me, he snapped, "I'm not Conor Cussane."

I blinked and took a step back, my calves pressing against the bed frame.

The King stared at me—or through me, perhaps—as if still stuck on the dead man's last words. Finally, he blinked, shook his head, and refocused on me, his expression softening as he returned to the present moment.

"Are you okay?" The King pushed off the dead man and stood, his scrutiny sweeping my naked body for the first time. But not with lust, with concern.

I nodded, unable to form words.

When his jaw hardened to granite as he noticed the scratches down my thighs, I shook my head. *No, they didn't get that far.*

An exhale escaped him, and something that resembled relief shone in his eyes.

The King closed the door as quickly and quietly as he could, considering the shape it was in from his kicking it open.

I stared at the dead bodies on the floor, blood streaming from their mouths and noses. Blood was everywhere.

More noise came from somewhere down the hall.

Shit.

The King quickly pulled a small pair of bolt cutters from his pants pocket and snapped the chain that bound me to the bed.

"I need you to run," he whispered as he removed the cuff. "Out the window, and run as fast as you can into the jungle."

"The jungle? W—where?"

"Run north, straight from the window. I'll find you." He took my hand and pulled me across the room.

"But I'm naked." I yanked out of his hold, as if my nudity was what mattered at that moment.

The King was one step ahead of me, picking up the jacket that had been tossed onto the floor. "Quickly."

He held open the suit jacket as I slipped into the sleeves.

He jerked open the window. "Run, now. And I need you to be quiet. Not a word," he said. "Can you do that, Samantha?"

He knew my name—my *real* name. Not my number.

I nodded, and to this day, I don't know why I trusted him so much. I don't know why I trusted a man who I knew had some sort of leadership position in this fucked-up world. A man who allowed children to be held captive, who watched women get their fingers clipped off.

A man who awoke every sexual sensor in my body.

The King hoisted me into the frame of the window. "Quiet," he whispered in my ear, guiding my body onto the ground outside. "*Go.*"

I stumbled on the launch forward, my legs struggling to remember how to run. Digging my bare toes into the wet earth, I took off like a bullet, sprinting into the pitch-black jungle in the middle of the night wearing nothing but a suit jacket.

I remember hearing shouts. I remember a spotlight illuminating me.

But mostly, I remember the crack of the gunshot.

20

*T*he first bullet missed me by inches. The second ricocheted off a tree just above my head, sending an explosion of bark into the air.

I ran blindly, full force, through the dense foliage like a wild animal. Rocks and stones cut my bare feet. Thorny bushes and twigs dragged like switchblades over my naked body, continually snagging on my suit jacket as I sprinted past.

Though the moon was full, the thick canopy of leaves overhead blocked the light, stealing any hope I had for a sense of direction.

Straight. Just stay straight, I reminded myself, focusing on placing each foot directly in front of the other so that I didn't deviate from the path.

"I'll find you."

The vegetation became thicker, the terrain more uneven, threatening to trip me with each step, yet my speed didn't slow. I was running for my life, running from the hell that had enslaved me for weeks.

I fell twice, tumbling painfully to the ground, only to use that momentum to push back up and begin again.

As I ran into the jungle, I began to fear not only the men who were probably chasing me, but also the jungle that was closing in around me, suffocating me. The sounds of nature intensified around me, a concert of thrumming and buzzing and chirping. It was so loud, I wouldn't be able to hear someone coming after me.

I ran, and ran, and ran, clumsily bouncing off trees, pushing through bushes, leaping over fallen trees.

Stay straight, stay straight.

Sweat poured down my face, dripping off the tip of my nose. I could barely breathe in the humid air.

The gunshots stopped, the voices and shouts faded in the distance.

Still, I ran.

Adrenaline, and adrenaline alone, was what kept me going that night. I'd had nothing but a stale muffin and a cup of water that day. Combining that with the weight loss and sedentary life of being kept in a cage, it was nothing short of a miracle I made it as far as I did.

After what felt like an hour, fatigue began to take hold. My legs were past the burning and tingling phase, and well into the almost-giving-out phase. I finally allowed myself to slow and began hiking upward, crawling over massive boulders, slipping between narrow crevices of stone.

The trees thinned, silver beams of moonlight dappling the jungle floor ahead.

I stopped suddenly, getting the feeling that I wasn't alone.

Knowing I wasn't alone.

Out of nowhere, it seemed, an arm wrapped around my waist and a hand clamped over my mouth. I was lifted off the ground, my body spun, and I was shoved backward into the ledge of a cliff, between two beams of moonlight splashed like paint against the rocks.

"Quiet," the King whispered into my ear.

I sucked in air through my nose, trying to control my heaving breaths. My heart felt like it was about to explode.

"Quiet," he said again, then slowly lowered his hand from my mouth. Streaks of moonlight slashed his face, twinkling in his green eyes. "Stay here."

He didn't wait for a response, simply left me hugging a cliff, half-naked like a woman on the stake.

I focused on the light pat of his footsteps over rocks, the rustle of leaves somewhere nearby, and then . . . nothing.

My eyes rounded as I desperately tried to see anything in the darkness in front of me.

Silence engulfed me.

Seconds passed. Minutes.

I thought he'd left me, when suddenly, his hand gripped mine, the touch like a bolt of lightning through my body. He guided me around the edge of the cliff—then pulled me into it. The temperature dropped quickly, the heavy humidity replaced with cool, crisp air scented with damp earth.

A cave.

Intermittent flashes of moonlight danced along the rock wall, illuminating the mouth of a tiny crevice that speared into the cliff. The space was so narrow that we could only fit in one at a time.

The King pulled me along, guiding me deeper as my eyes adjusted to inky blackness and random flashes of moonlight.

We stopped and he turned, put his hands on my naked waist, and pulled me to him, our bodies pressing together as he wedged around me. My skin ignited with the touch of his.

With his hands on my shoulders, he guided me backward until my back was against the end of the cave, his body solidly blocking mine from the opening. Again I was trapped, but this time I believed it was for my safety.

Following his lead, I froze and held my breath as he appeared to be listening for something.

Finally, he said, "Sit." When I did, he shifted his stance where he could see both me and the cave entrance in his peripheral vision.

I stared at the silhouette of his face. "Who are you?" I whispered into the darkness.

He was a massive black outline looming over my half-naked body.

"My name is Roman Thieves. I'm here to save you."

21

*W*ell, *fuck.*

Never deviate from the plan. And yet I'd deviated *the fuck* from that plan.

I was supposed to get Sam alone, ask her about the USB, wait for Conor's arrival, buy her, then hand her off to Bear, who would deliver her home.

Then I would deal with the son of the man who'd killed my mother.

I hadn't planned on the guards lingering outside the bedroom door like the horny fucking bastards they were. I hadn't planned on them sneaking back in while I'd met secretly with Lucas in a separate wing of the lodge. I hadn't planned on the uncontrollable rage that consumed me when I saw them on top of her.

And most of all, I hadn't planned on fucking *killing* them.

Fucking *Christ.*

"You are Conor Cussane." Four words I'd also never planned on hearing.

What the fuck? Why did the guard think I was Conor Cussane?

"*They all know,*" he'd said.

Who? Who knew what? Who thought I was the leader of the CUN?

And *why*? Where had they gotten that idea?

These questions would have to wait as I had another, more pressing, much more beautiful matter to deal with.

After Bear had taken out the rooftop shooter from his perch on the cliff, and I was certain Samantha had made it safely into the jungle, I'd eliminated the guard who'd seen everything from the hallway, tossing his body out the window and dragging him—and the rooftop shooter—into a nearby utility shed before taking off after her. Two dead bodies remained in the room. I couldn't risk the time it would take to hide those bodies. And even then, how could I? Blood was everywhere.

Bear and I had lost contact after the shooting. I assumed he was repositioning his post closer to the lodge—and reloading, for that matter. I didn't care. My sole focus was getting to Samantha.

Four men were dead—three by my own hands— blowing my plan to shit. Soon, legions of Conor Cussane's men would be combing the woods, searching for Samantha Greene.

What would happen if they found her? I couldn't fathom what those evil motherfuckers would deem as her punishment.

Another thought—what would happen if they saw me with her? My cover would be blown. Decades of working tirelessly to infiltrate the CUN would be for nothing. My entire life's work thrown out the window. For *her*.

It was an absolute clusterfuck.

I'd told her I was there to save her. *Ha.* What *the fuck* was I thinking?

I hadn't been thinking, and that was the problem.

When I saw the men on her, it was like a switch flipped inside me, an indescribable fury overtaking all rational thought. I turned into an animal, completely uncontrollable, despite years of practice to tame my destructive temper. After years of lying dormant, the lion inside me awoke, and I attacked.

Protecting what was mine.

Except she wasn't. Samantha Greene was one of hundreds of slaves I'd walked past, avoided eye contact with, ignored, while building my cover. It was my *job* to watch the horrors of human trafficking unfold, and that included torture and rape. It was my job because that was the only way I was going to end it. To gain access to the man at the top, to cut the head off the snake.

What *the fuck* had I been thinking?

What was it about this woman that consumed me so much? Why? And why her?

Samantha Greene was a divorcee—from Oklahoma, for fuck's sake—who wore Crocs on the weekends, drove a car with a bumper sticker that read MAKE TACOS, NOT WAR, and spent her evenings sleeping with a dog that drooled like an infant and looked like Chewbacca.

I'm here to save you.

How? How could I do that now? I couldn't give this woman what she needed. I had two skill sets: killing and getting the job done. I was one for two on this mission.

What the hell was I thinking? Everything had gone to shit because I couldn't control myself when it came to her.

Her . . . her . . . *her.*

Fuck her.

I wouldn't allow *her* to wreck this for me. I could not, would not, blow my cover. I couldn't waste this opportunity —*the* opportunity—to avenge my mother.

Samantha Greene wouldn't stand in my way. I was so close, so goddamn close.

I decided then that I hated her.

So, why the fuck did I want to pull her onto my lap, wrap her in my arms, and hold her until she stopped looking at me that way?

Why did I want to make love to her more than I wanted my next breath?

22

ROMAN

"*R*oman . . . Thieves?" Samantha repeated in a soft whisper, my name rolling like silk from those lips.

God*damn* those lips.

The cave was pitch dark, but with just enough moonlight streaming in to make out her features, her gaze pinned on me. My body tensed, reacting to her apparent fear. I wasn't good at this.

I stared at the cave wall with no response, nothing more than an animal incapable of handling anything that didn't involve life or death.

No, I wasn't good at this shit.

This wasn't the fucking plan.

"You're not Conor Cussane?"

"No." I turned my face away from her, wishing she weren't there. That she wouldn't speak, wouldn't make me feel so damn—

"Then why did the guard call you that?"

"Never trust the words from a dying man's lips."

"I thought it was the opposite . . . that a man is never more honest than when he's dying."

"You don't believe me?" I asked.

The question lingered. Answer enough.

A long moment stretched between us.

"You're Irish," she said eventually.

So, she'd noticed my accent. I suddenly felt like I was losing the anonymity I'd so carefully crafted. I didn't want her to know me.

"Ardri means *high king* in Gaelic, I know this," she said. "Why do they call you that?"

"Because they don't know better. Hush. We need to be quiet." I closed the few feet between us and reached behind her.

When she flinched, I froze. Blinked. Stared back at her.

It was then that I realized that I wasn't the only one unsettled by the situation we'd found ourselves in. Although I'd rescued her from being raped by two drunk animals, Samantha didn't trust me.

For a second, I actually thought she was going to attack me, right there in the cave. And I wanted her to, I realized. It would make this easier. Make me hate her. Redirect my attention away from her and back to the mission at hand— delivering her to Bear, then going after Conor.

A beam of moonlight caught her face, her narrowed eyes active, flickering like an animal backed against a wall.

Watching her, I yanked loose the small pack I'd hidden in the cave two days earlier when I'd mapped out my exit route. *My* exit route—intended for *after* I'd handed Samantha Greene off to Bear. I dropped the pack in her lap.

She gave me a confused look. "What's this?"

"Survival pack."

"You . . . you planted this here?"

"Yes."

"When?"

I ignored the question, growing annoyed by her interrogation.

"You knew this was going to happen?" she asked.

I knew *I* was eventually going to need it—not *us*.

Samantha set the bag aside and refocused on me in a way that reminded me of my supervisor in basic training. "Who are you?" she asked, a bit of sharpness to her tone.

"I told you—"

"No, *who* are you, Roman? Are you in the military?"

"Not anymore."

"Do you work for the US government?"

"No."

"Do you work for the Mexican government?"

"No."

"The Irish government?"

"No."

"Roman, who do—"

"I work for Astor Stone, Inc., a private military contracting firm. And I told you we need to be quiet—"

"What do you do for them?"

I released a pained growl.

"Answer me," she said tersely. "What do you do for this Astor Stone?"

"Take orders."

"You mean, like, black ops stuff?"

"Yeah, like black ops stuff."

Her expression soured in disapproval of my mocking tone. Yet still, she pressed on with her questions.

"Like a James Bond or Jason Bourne type of thing?"

"James Bond and Jason Bourne are fictional characters."

"And you're not. So, what are you? A mercenary?"

I wasn't into labels. Despised them almost as much as questions.

She snorted. "A mercenary," she said again, letting it soak in. "So, you get paid to kill people then, yes?"

"I get paid to handle shit."

"Who pays you?"

"My boss."

"Who pays him?"

"That's classified."

"The US government?"

No response.

"I'm right, aren't I?"

No response.

"Why did you hide this pack here?"

"Stop talking." I knelt down and reached for the bag, and when she flinched again, I snapped, "Stop doing that. I'm not going to hurt you."

"Why?"

"Because I don't hurt women."

"No. You just watch them being hurt."

A spark of anger flew through me. "I don't hurt women, Samantha. And you don't know a goddamn thing about me or why I do what I do." I unzipped the pack and wrestled out a T-shirt and a pair of lightweight all-weather pants. "Here."

The clothes were snatched from my hand like a starving child would a loaf of bread.

"Turn around," she demanded.

I turned my face away but remained crouched in front of her. I listened to the rustle of fabric as she slipped into the clothes and resettled on the cave floor. Then a long, deep, exhale.

I turned back to the pack, but not before sneaking a

glance at her.

My suit jacket had been folded neatly and placed on a nearby rock. The gray T-shirt swallowed her small frame, the thin fabric draping over a pair of erect nipples and perky round breasts. The pants were many sizes too large, but she'd found the drawstring around the waist and had cinched them tight. The cuffs she'd rolled above her small, delicate ankles. Chipped pink nail polish speckled her dirty toenails.

Our eyes met. Something crackled between us.

I tore my gaze away and began inventorying the bag I'd originally packed for one, mentally counting how many days of survival it now allowed for two.

Samantha watched me closely, unmoving, her back against the wall, a sharp rock now clutched in a death grip in her fist.

"Why?" she asked suddenly. "Why me?"

"What do you mean, why you?"

"Why me? Why save me?"

"I didn't think I needed your approval to be removed from a gang rape."

"I'm not the only one being gang-raped in that house."

"You're the only one I was tasked to save."

"What?"

I pulled a canteen of water from the pack and shoved it at her. "Drink."

"What do you mean, you were tasked to save *only* me?"

I shook the canteen. "Drink."

She took it and threw it against the wall. Surprised, I cocked a brow.

Samantha folded her arms over her chest. "What's going on?"

"You've got one hell of an attitude on you, considering your position less than an hour ago."

"That's *why* I have one hell of an attitude on me, you fucking idiot."

Touché.

"Roman, tell me—"

"The United States government hired me to save you."

Save—that word again. *Fuck.*

"The government?" Her eyes popped in disbelief. "Why? I'm just a schoolteacher—there are American *children* there that need to be saved!" Her voice tightened with emotion. "Why the hell me? The *children* need to be saved—why *me*?"

"Because you have information that could take down the entire network, thereby saving not only the children but hundreds of other slaves."

"Information? What information?"

"Conor Cussane, have you met him?"

She frowned. "That's the name the dying man called you."

"Yes. But I'm not him, as I've already told you. Did you meet anyone named Conor Cussane during your captivity?"

"I don't know . . . I mean, I don't think so."

She didn't know? What the fuck did she mean, she didn't know?

"The name sounded familiar when the guard said it."

"How familiar?"

"I heard the name from the guards a few times," she said. "I gathered that he was someone of importance, but . . . that's all."

"Do you mean to tell me that you've really never even met the man?"

"Not that I'm aware, no."

What the *fuck*? Was the intel of her being taken as

Conor's personal slave and future wife wrong? How could that be?

I shook my head. There was no fucking way.

"I need to repeat this, and I need you to really think hard. Samantha, in the two weeks you've been missing, you've never met a Conor Cussane?"

"No—I . . . no. Not that I know of, no."

"Was there one man that showed a particular interest in you?"

"No . . . no, they all treated me the same. Like dirt."

I regarded her closely for the first time, questioning her honesty. I'd been told the intel that she'd been taken as his personal slave was solid. Yet she hadn't met him? Or had she, and was protecting the monster for some crazy reason?

"I don't understand," she said, her thoughts obviously spinning. "What are you asking me?"

"Did you see a USB drive at any time during your captivity?"

"A USB drive?"

"A thumb drive, whatever. Any kind of computer data storage device?"

She thought for a moment. "No. I was rarely let out of my cage."

"What about the guards? Did you ever see any of the men holding one?"

"No."

"Did you see a computer? A laptop? Did you see anything like that?"

"No." Frustration boiled in her tone. "I don't know what you're talking about. I was held in a damn cage in a basement. I never saw anything like that."

Truth? Or lies? I wondered.

If truth, what led the government to think Samantha

had been taken as Conor's personal slave? And why *the hell* had one of the guards thought *I* was Conor Cussane?

Something—lots of things—weren't adding up.

"What about the other slaves at the lodge? Who's going to save them?" she asked, pulling me back to the current moment.

"I'm working on it."

"Work faster." Her chin lifted, defiant, defensive. Ready for a fight. No, there was absolutely nothing extremely emotional and mentally fragile about Samantha Greene.

"Fast is messy. I'll do what I can."

"How can I help?" she asked.

Staring at her, I frowned, utterly confused by this woman.

How can she help? She wanted to go back and help the other slaves, instead of saving herself?

"There are two American children," she said quickly while she knew she had my attention. "A boy and a girl. Twins, I think. You've seen them. They were brought in the day you came to the other house."

What a monster this woman must think I am. What a fool she is.

"There's something wrong with the boy," she said desperately. "I think he has a medical condition. They need out. They're too young . . . They need your help."

I realized then that Samantha had no clue that everyone in the lodge was scheduled to be on a boat in six days, shipped to Africa, and never be seen or heard from again.

"I told you I'm working on it." I pushed to my feet and began pacing, my frustration with how *off* this mission had gone coming to a boiling point.

"It's not enough," she snapped back. "We have to go back and get them. We have to—"

"Get us both killed in the process?" I barked back. "Who would save them then?"

A tense silence settled between us.

"We have to get them," she said again stubbornly.

"How about I get you out of this mess first." I gestured to the jungle outside the cave. "Then I'll focus on the others."

"Where are we?"

"The Sierra Madre Mountains, in an area known as Dead Man's Trail. I have a plane on standby at a small hanger forty-seven miles north of here. It's ready to take you home as soon as you arrive. I just have to get you there."

I just have to get her there. Dump her with Bear, revise my plan, return to my focus, and never see this distraction again.

Just get her there.

23

SAM

Take you home.

Home—the single word was like a punch to my chest. Tears welled in my eyes, a rush of emotions threatening to take over.

I couldn't break down in front of this man. I couldn't think about home—not yet. I pushed it away, the sudden visions of my mother, my dog, my bed, my shower, my *real* life, for fear the emotion would weaken me. I needed to be alert and ready, focused solely on survival and not on home.

I fidgeted with the hem of the T-shirt Roman had given me. It smelled like him.

I realized then that clothing—clean clothes—was one of the little things in life that I'd taken for granted before my captivity . . . one among *so* many. The moment my bare skin was covered and concealed, it felt like I'd been given a shot of courage. I felt less vulnerable, more confident, more *me*.

The *old* me.

I didn't know who I'd become, but I knew that if I made it out of this jungle alive, I would emerge a completely different woman.

The pants had multiple pockets down each leg, now filled with every sharp rock within reaching distance. The hip pocket hid my newly deformed hand—the one that made me feel weak. My other hand was wrapped around a pointed rock in a vise-like grip.

Roman Thieves was a man of many secrets, this much was evident. But for some reason, I knew in my gut that Roman wasn't a danger to me. Something deep in my soul confirmed this. I had no fear toward him, but that didn't mean I shouldn't be prepared.

Roman pulled something from the pack, shifted his weight, and grabbed my ankle. This startled me, and I kicked instinctively, slamming my big toe dead center into his nose.

"Shit!" he bellowed, jerking back. "Holy—*Jesus!*" He scrunched his face, squeezing shut his eyes that were now streaming with tears.

"I'm sorry," I said quickly, but with zero sincerity.

"Dammit, woman." He bit out the words, swiping away the tears and checking the back of his hand for blood.

"I said I'm sorry." I pulled my knees to my chest.

Squinting through the tears, he wiped his cheeks again, then held out his palm. "Give me your goddamn foot."

"Why?"

"Listen—I'm not doing this with you right now. Trust me or don't, I don't give a shit, but make that decision right now. Either you trust me and do as I say, or you don't, and I will let you to leave this cave right now."

I blinked, staring back, unsure how to respond. There was no way I could survive in the jungle alone.

"Which is it?" he asked impatiently.

Slowly, I unfolded my leg.

Roman grabbed my ankle, then began tending to the

wounds on the bottom of my bare feet from sprinting across the jungle floor. It hurt, it stung, it tickled, it turned me on.

My cheeks heated.

God, this *man*.

"They're going to be sore," he said, applying the final Band-Aid. "But you don't need stitches." Then he pulled ACE bandages from the pack and began wrapping each foot.

"They're not sprained," I said.

"Shoes," he said. "This will have to do for now. My shoes are too big and will only trip you up. This will protect your feet enough during the day. We'll take them off and let them dry out at night."

At night . . .

When he reached for the other leg, I instinctively jerked again, then winced. "*Dammit.* Sorry."

Roman stared at me a moment, then seemed to decide something. He reached into the pack and tossed me a knife. "Here."

I stared at the sheathed knife that had landed on my lap. It was a hunting knife of sorts, the kind you would gut an animal with.

"It'll weigh less than those rocks you stuffed in your pockets when you thought I wasn't watching. Do you know how to use it?"

"Yes."

He peered up under his lashes, securing the bandages. "In a fight, I mean."

"Oh. Uh, no."

He nodded as if he'd expected this and was equally disappointed. "You understand, Samantha, that once the men realize you escaped, they'll comb this jungle to find you. They won't stop until they find and kill you. You've seen too many faces."

My eyes rounded. I'd been so focused on escaping that I hadn't considered that I would be hunted.

"They've probably already started searching," he said, glancing over his shoulder.

"But you said you killed them."

"Not all of them, and I wasn't able to get rid of all the bodies."

"They have to know *I* didn't kill those men . . ."

He shrugged. "No way to know right now. I'd rather be prepared, wouldn't you?" He refocused on the knife. "Knives are useless in self-defense unless you hit a vital organ or artery. That is always your goal, do you understand?"

I nodded, shifting my focus back to survival.

"You're short, five-foot-four, I'm guessing, and therefore will probably always be smaller than your attacker. Use that against him. Your height is not a weakness."

He gently set down my foot, stood, and began demonstrating.

"Always keep the tip of your blade pointed at your attacker, not to the side—not all limp-dick at your hip like an imbecile. Don't look around for help like an idiot, stay focused on him, and him only. You are preparing for attack —never assume otherwise. You fight, Samantha, *fight*."

Roman stepped behind a tall, thin rock spearing up from the cave.

"Put an obstacle between you and him, and keep the point of the blade aligned on the attacker. *Always* keep your body behind your knife. When he advances, don't be a pussy and slash like a girl. You want to stab hard, stab downward, and twist the blade if you can. Leave the blade and run if you got him good."

"Do you always talk to women like this?"

"I rarely talk to women."

"I see."

Roman fisted his hands on his hips, glowering at me. "You've quite the attitude, you know that?"

"You've told me this already."

He shook his head, then returned to the subject. "Never stand flat-footed, always on your toes, always moving..." He pointed the knife at me. "...while doing what?"

"Keeping the knife between me and the man."

"Right. Good job. Keep your body small and tight, your limbs close together, not flailing about like a—"

"Idiot. Got it." I rolled my eyes. "Keep going."

"Never use your other arm as a shield. This is the most common mistake. It opens your body for attack. And never extend your arm fully while stabbing."

"But you said it yourself, I'll be smaller than my attacker. I'd have to fully extend my arm."

"No. Get in close. It's the opposite of what he'll expect. Move in after dodging a blow or follow your attacker's arms as he retracts after a punch. Stay low, go in like a fucking lion, get it done, get out."

Like a fucking lion. A surge of adrenaline pumped through my veins at that thought.

Gripping the knife tightly, I turned it over in my hands, examining the lines, the length. It felt good. It made me feel like I had some control back, that I could do something. All of a sudden, I felt strong.

Strong like a lion. *Like a fucking lion.*

"Thank you." I spoke before thinking it through. "For what you did—for saving me. Killing those men."

"Give me your hand," he said, ignoring my gratitude. Or uncomfortable with it, perhaps.

I lifted my right arm.

"No. The other hand." Roman knelt at my feet. "The hand that's in your pocket."

I hesitated. "You—you already saw it. In the room."

He opened his palm, impatiently waggling his fingers.

Swallowing hard, I pulled my disfigured hand from my pocket, clenching my fist so he couldn't see the grotesque nub that once was my pinky finger.

He took my hand and opened my palm with surprising gentleness. Examined the nub again, for infection, I assumed.

"They did it after I acted out, shortly after kidnapping me," I whispered.

"No," he said, "they did it to trick the authorities. They used your bones as a diversion, to make everyone think you were dead."

Stunned, I blinked at him. "They'd told me that no one was looking for me anymore, but I didn't realize . . ."

Roman ran the tip of his finger along the inside of my bruised, dirty, skinny wrist.

The humiliation dissolved the rush of confidence I'd felt moments earlier.

He leaned in even closer.

Peeking from under my lashes, I was startled at what I saw. Roman's face was flushed, his jaw hardened to razor-sharp edges. The veins in his neck were bulging, his lips twitching.

"It's fine." I pulled my hand away and stuffed it into my lap.

Our eyes met, mine fighting tears, his so intense that goose bumps rippled my arms.

"You're beautiful," he said, completely out of nowhere and with no emotion whatsoever.

I frowned. "What?"

"You're beautiful."

Roman lifted his chin. His face was fierce, his green eyes daring me to object.

My brows pulled together in confusion. The comment didn't seem so much of a compliment, but more a way to ensure that I was simply aware of the fact.

Thanks?

"Okay," I said slowly.

He dipped his chin—conversation over—then pulled another canteen out of the pack, along with two MREs. "Now, eat."

Food. I sat up with a surge of excitement.

He ripped the top off the MRE and placed the contents in front of me. My mouth watered.

As I ripped into the tiny bags, Roman ignored his. Instead, he perched on a rock and began sharpening a knife he kept in his boot.

The food was surprisingly good, or perhaps it was just because it was the first time I'd eaten outside of a cage in two weeks. I was starving, I realized, and had to force myself to slow down so that I wouldn't get a stomachache.

"Is that your only wound?" he asked, apparently still thinking about the finger that I just wanted to forget about.

"Yes."

"You haven't been branded?"

I coughed, choking on a dehydrated-something. "Branded?"

"Yes. The CUN brands its slaves before being sold. On the inside of the wrist, they carve the letter *C*."

My stomach rolled. "Oh my God . . . No. No, I haven't been branded."

"Good."

When I didn't respond, he jerked his chin to the food, indicating that I keep eating. I forced my focus on my food once again.

"You said we're in the Sierra Madre Mountains?" I asked around something that tasted like cardboard but crumbled like cheese.

"Yes, on Dead Man's Trail."

"So, how are we getting to the airport?"

"Our feet."

"*What*?" A crumb dropped from my chin, and I snapped my mouth closed.

"What?" he asked.

"We're *walking* to the airport? Through the jungle?"

"Well, I had a driver lined up to take us, but I've lost contact after—"

"After you went and killed two men who planned to rape me."

He nodded, and I wondered if he regretted this decision.

"Okay . . ." I took a deep breath, then sighed. "You said forty-seven miles?"

"Correct—to a small town called Tenedores. We'll catch a ride to the airport from there."

"Sooo . . . how long is forty-seven miles in terms of days?"

"With you, four days."

Four days?

Four days in the jungle with nothing but a canteen of water, a few MREs, and bandages for my feet?

Four days, three nights.

Three nights with this man. Alone. In these woods.

Unsure what to say next, I settled back and ate the food while Roman manically sharpened a blade that no doubt could already cut through steel.

A monkey screamed somewhere in the distance. Shadows danced like ghosts along the dark cave walls.

"You know I did a paper on this trail in high school," I said. "This area is supposed to be haunted. It was named the scariest haunted hiking trail in Mexico by a popular travel magazine."

"I know."

Of course he did.

"Do you also know that this particular area is said to be haunted by a child?"

Roman shot me a look, the closest thing to an eye roll that his masculinity allowed.

"That's the legend. Rumor is, thirty years ago, a seven-year-old child was abducted from his family's campsite after he wandered off to use the bathroom. His body was found two days later—his carcass, I should say. His torso had been split open and his organs had been removed."

I paused for a reaction. When I got none from this stone-cold man, I continued.

"Initially, they thought he'd been eaten by bears, until they realized the cuts were too clean and the organs had been severed by a sharp tool, like a knife. Someone had stolen this kid, cut him open, and eaten his insides. Since then, there have been at least five instances of carcasses of multiple animals—and one woman—found with their organs removed the same way. One hiker says he woke up to a child standing outside his tent with a blank expression, with his insides spilling out. And multiple hikers have reported hearing a child's scream in the night. The legend is, the kid still haunts this area until his killer is found."

"Are you done?"

"Scary, isn't it?"

"It's ridiculous."

"You don't believe in ghosts?"

"No."

"*That's* ridiculous."

"Is it?"

"Yes," I said defiantly, like a child. "I absolutely believe in a higher power, and that there's much more happening in this world beyond what we can see and touch."

"Ghosts? Seriously?"

"I believe that spirits walk among us, those with unfinished business of sorts."

"That's a lot of spirts, then."

"Not all haunt. Some are just waiting for their time to redeem themselves . . . something I get the feeling you know a lot about."

He said nothing.

I tipped up my MRE, sucking something that resembled mashed sweet potatoes from a hole at the top.

"I was never raped or beaten," I said, as emotionless as if we were speaking about the weather. "It was like they were saving me for something. Do you know why? Why was I spared?"

"Intel suggested that Conor, the leader of the organization that kidnapped you, had chosen you to bear his children, be his future wife. One of many, I should say."

I gasped, the thought of being forced to have sex with an evil monster and bear his children was absolutely unimaginable. The thought that I'd have to live this life for that long was even worse. Honestly, I didn't think it would be long until I was killed. Believe it or not, I'd taken solace in that.

Roman watched me closely, appearing to be gauging my reaction.

"We have to save those kids, Roman," I said, my stomach now churning.

"Focus on now, Samantha. Now."

I leaned my head against the cold cave wall behind me and watched him for a bit.

"So," I asked a few minutes later, "are you the good guys or the bad guys?"

"What?"

"Astor Stone . . . the company you work for. Are you the good or the bad guys?"

"A little of both," he said quietly. Honestly.

"How many mercenaries does Astor Stone employ?"

"There are four of us."

"Four?"

"That's right."

"Doesn't seem like a lot for saving the world."

"We're not saving the world. We're following orders and getting paid to follow those orders. Our job is the mission we get assigned, and the successful completion of that mission. That's it. Once the job is done, we're on to the next. And on and on it goes."

"Are you given information as to why you're being sent on the missions?"

"We receive what's necessary to complete the mission."

"You don't ask questions?"

"Not nearly as many as you do."

I snorted, the quip catching me off balance. "Sorry."

I chewed on my lower lip, replaying in my mind seeing Roman for the first time.

The guards *knew* him. They called him *the King*. Roman Thieves was respected within the trafficking community.

This was not just some in-and-out mission. This wasn't just about me, as he'd said. Roman would have had to work years on building his cover, his reputation. For what? What was his end goal?

I decided to poke. "So I, Samantha Greene, am this mission? *Only* me?"

He looked away. Yes, there was definitely more to the story than just me.

"You said the government hired you to save me, right?" I asked.

"Correct."

"Because they thought—incorrectly—that I knew where this USB thing is."

"They thought you might be able to provide valuable information, yes."

Lost in thought, I nibbled on something brown and chewy.

"Does my . . . mom know?" My voice cracked. "That I'm alive?"

"No."

Breath escaped me as I hunched forward, shaking my head, fighting the tears that came with the gut-wrenching guilt for how much pain I was causing her. "Oh my God, someone has to tell her. I can't imagine . . ."

"I'll get you home, Samantha. Soon. You'll tell her yourself."

I sniffed, mad at the emotions. I could feel him watching me.

"You two are close?" he asked.

"Yes." I angrily scrubbed my eyes, willing the pain away. "She used to . . . never mind, it's so stupid."

"Tell me."

"No, it's—"

"Please."

I frowned, trying to understand this rare show of an emotion that didn't involve anger, and the sudden interest in my relationship with my mother.

"When I was a little girl, she would sing 'Somewhere Over the Rainbow' to me. After I was kidnapped and put in the cage, singing that song in my head was the only thing that could console and calm me." I shook my head, waving my hand in the air as if to wave away the emotion. "Anyway. Yes, we're close. She's my everything."

Our eyes met.

Roman had leaned toward me, leaning in, hanging on my every word. "I'll get you home to your mother, Samantha Greene. I promise you that."

I pretended to examine the knife in my lap while forcing away the tears.

The knife. The fucking knife I'd been given to defend my life. The knife that I'd just been instructed how to use to kill someone.

What the fuck had I gotten myself into? Who was I?

"Sleep," he said softly, tucking a tangled strand of hair behind my ear. "Try to sleep."

That night, I pretended to sleep as Roman stood guard at the edge of the cave.

I pretended to sleep when he eventually settled in next to me.

I pretended to sleep as I rested my head on his shoulder.

I pretended to sleep as I focused on the inhale and exhale of his breath.

And for the first time in countless dark days, I slept while I felt safe.

24

"*G*et up."

I startled awake at the low, gravelly voice above me, and shot up into a seated position. Blinking wildly, I tried to discern the unfamiliar surroundings while my head was heavy with sleep.

I saw dark cave walls. Clothing, a million sizes too big. Bandaged feet.

Him.

Him—the mercenary. My savior.

"It's time to get moving," Roman said, organizing the pack.

Get moving? Ah yes, from the evil men who wanted me dead.

I nodded, then clumsily pushed off the cave floor, sore in places I didn't know existed from sprinting through the jungle.

He was a vision, a tall, wide, deliciously muscular body, backlit by the cave entrance.

Sometime in the night, Roman had changed out of his suit and into a thin gray T-shirt and tactical pants, matching the clothing he'd given me the day before. Except he filled out every inch of his clothing. A pair of worn, scuffed combat boots covered his feet. A handgun was secured in a holster resting on one hip, a long sheathed knife on the other. Ink swirled over his bare arms, full sleeves of interlocking tattoos that disappeared under the short sleeves.

I knew his chest was bare from when he'd unbuttoned in front of me while I was chained to the bed. And suddenly, I wanted to see the full picture.

Instead of the slick, rich, smooth-talking businessman he was at the lodge, Roman looked more like the mercenary he claimed to be. He was alert, ready, totally in his element.

While I, on the other hand, looked like a feral cat after being caught in a drain.

Despite being wobbly on my sore, ACE-bandaged feet, I squared my shoulders, lifted my chin, and forced confidence. "I'm ready."

The corner of his mouth quirked.

I blinked. *Is that a smile? Am I amusing him?*

Roman lifted a small copper cup that I hadn't noticed in his massive hand. "Let's start with this."

"What is it?"

"Coffee."

My jaw dropped. This time, his lips actually curved.

"Did you say coffee?" I said much too eagerly.

"So, you do drink . . ."

I lunged forward, grabbing the cup from his hand. "No. I chug."

Cupping the mug with both hands, I downed the contents in one go, uncaring that it was tepid, obviously instant, and tasted a bit like dirt. My body surged to life like a superhero being recharged.

I licked my lips, then smiled somewhat maniacally. I got a full, legitimate smile back, and even a bit of a chuckle.

"So you can smile," I teased.

"I can when I see that."

"You're welcome." I swiped my lips with the back of my hand.

"Come on, Juan Valdez. We've got a long day ahead of us."

We started out just before daybreak, after Roman erased any sign of our presence in the cave and then sprayed every inch of my body—including my hair—with bug spray. It stank, but I was thankful for this, hoping the strong scent masked the smell of my unwashed skin.

The morning was cool, the air ripe with the scent of dawn—fresh, earthy, floral. To my surprise, the bandages on my feet worked almost as well as shoes, padding and protecting my cuts from the rough terrain.

As the sun rose, the jungle was slowly illuminated in muted golden light. Dewdrops shimmered on large banana leaves, and birds sang loudly as if greeting the morning. Life was all around us, even in the trees and bushes, a steady white noise of energy humming through the jungle.

Color was also all around us, bright pops of pink and red exotic flowers, luminescent shades of shimmering green, yellow, and orange birds, hopping from branch to branch. I even saw a blue frog—yes, bright blue, like the sky above.

It truly was beautiful, and I made a promise to myself that I would never take another morning for granted.

Roman, on the other hand, was entirely focused, following a path he seemed to know by heart. There was a sense of urgency in his step, one that kept me checking over my shoulder every few minutes.

We hiked silently through the rugged terrain, him

leading with me exactly one foot from his side, as he'd demanded. He carried me over the terrain when it got too rocky for my injured feet, held my hand through the rushing streams of cool water, and guided me down steep valleys and narrow gorges. When I needed a break, he let me rest; when I was hungry, eat. The only thing he wouldn't do was speak.

His mind constantly raced. I could see it in the crease of his brow, the way he held his jaw. Internally tormented, fighting a war inside his head. And oh how I wanted a peek inside the mind of Roman Thieves.

We stopped exactly once an hour, Roman instructing me where to stand. Usually on a tree root, with my back against the thick base of the tree. I figured this was some sort of safety measure. Meanwhile, he retraced our steps and covered our tracks. Then we continued on.

The temperature rose quickly, the comfortable morning air quickly replaced with thick and sticky humidity. Even under the shade of the trees, the air was stifling, and my skin was wet with sweat before the sun fully rose.

Bugs buzzed around us. I'd never seen so many swarms of flying insects in my life.

Roman swatted through the swarms of bugs, clearing a path for me. Still, they targeted my eyes, nose, and mouth. Eventually, I gave up on trying to swat them away. We were in their territory, after all.

The jungle was alive with activity, ignoring, or perhaps laughing at us there in its territory. I felt so small in its presence. Vulnerable.

Growing up near the Ouachita Mountains, I'd hiked many times, but never like this. There was a feeling of true isolation in the jungle. We were nothing but insignificant specks in this wild, untamed wilderness.

My feet throbbed with pain. My stomach growled with hunger. The protein bar Roman had given me during one of our breaks had quickly metabolized in my malnourished, fatigued, overheated body. I knew we had very little food and water, so I didn't ask for more than I was allotted.

I grew weak and weary but was too proud to ask him to stop.

The hours dragged on and on, the temperature and humidity rising to suffocating levels. I was drenched in sweat. At one point, I actually considered telling him to go on without me. I'd find my way or die trying. At least then I would die on my own terms instead of in a dog cage next to other slaves.

My knees began to shake, my vision suddenly wavering. I stumbled on a tree root, my body lurching forward like dead weight.

Roman spun like lightning. Two arms wrapped around me as I began to tip. He lowered me to the ground.

The words *don't vomit, don't vomit, don't vomit all over this guy* swirled through my dazed mind.

He gently guided me onto my back, then raised my knees. He checked my pulse, pinched the thin skin of the back of my hand, then pressed and examined the tips of my fingers, although I had no clue what he was checking for.

"I'm sorry," I whispered, embarrassed by my weakness.

Roman didn't respond, simply slid his arms under me, scooped me into his arms, and carried me off the invisible trail to a thicket of ferns.

I let go in his arms, releasing my weight, my armor. I knew I was wet with sweat, but I didn't care. I stank, but I didn't care. Honestly, right then and there, I didn't care if the world swallowed me up and took me away forever.

I was lowered again onto the forest floor, this time on a

bed of cool, dewy fern leaves. It felt like heaven, and I closed my eyes.

My head was lifted, water trickled into my mouth. I swallowed, reveling in the cool rush down my throat.

"I'm so sorry," I said again, staring up at him. "I'm so embarrassed."

"You've gone seven miles longer than I expected you to today. I shouldn't have pushed you so hard."

"No. No. I'm just . . ."

"I know."

Our eyes met, a moment of softness in his. Of understanding.

Of respect.

"We'll take a break here." He scanned the area, confirming the safety of our hiding spot. "Eat, rest a minute."

I closed my eyes as something cool dabbed my forehead.

To my absolute shock, that was the last thing I remember. I fell asleep, right there on the jungle floor, exhaustion literally overtaking me.

25

I awoke to a beam of sunlight scorching my eyelids. Though my body pulsed with heat, something cool and wet lay over my forehead.

I sat up, a wet sock tumbling to my lap, and immediately locked eyes with Roman, looming over me like a sentinel.

"Oh my—I fell asleep?" Blinking, I ran my fingers through my sweaty hair.

"Do you feel better?"

"Yes . . . yes, a lot."

"You look a lot better."

"Didn't take much, I'm sure."

Roman knelt next to me and gently handed me the canteen. "Drink—please . . . please drink."

I blinked, noting the sudden shift from his cold, stoic demeanor, as if he were suddenly making an effort to be more patient. The word *please* was obviously uncomfortable and foreign to him.

It was endearing.

Roman watched me closely as I drank from the canteen. Once satisfied with my consumption, he took the water from my hands, set it aside, then unwrapped a granola bar and lifted it to my lips. "Please eat."

"Please?" I bit off the tip and chewed.

"Thank you."

My brows arched. "Please and thank you . . ." I swallowed the gooey morsels. "Did you attend a Gary Chapman lecture while I was asleep?"

"Who's Gary Chapman?" Roman asked disinterestedly, his full focus on feeding me another bite.

His hair was mussed in a sexy, bedhead kind of way. His eyes were alert, solely focused on me. I noticed the little lines around his eyes, and the beginnings of deeper ones on his forehead. The gray threads at his temples, in his thickening five-o'clock shadow.

Roman was all man. Strong, confident, and intimidating in the sexiest way. I wondered what he thought of my age. If it mattered to him. If I mattered to him.

And what a crazy thought.

"*The Five Love Languages*, the bestselling book . . ." I paused as I was force-fed another chunk of granola. "He's the author." I stared at Roman's blank expression. "You have no idea . . . okay, then. Anyway . . ."

"There are *five* love languages?" he asked, bewildered by this.

"Yes." I swallowed a laugh. "Words of affirmation, gifts, acts of service, quality time, and physical touch."

His brow cocked with a sudden interest in the subject. "Define acts of service."

"Not like that, you pervert."

When a grin tugged at the corner of his mouth, little bubbles of excitement tickled my stomach. God, I loved to make him smile.

I took the granola from his hand, feeling a renewed rush

of energy. Feeling like a totally different person.

I regarded him closely. "Based on your immediate interest in acts of service, I'm going to say your love language is number five, physical touch."

"Every man's language is physical touch."

"Not true."

"I'm willing to place a bet on this one, Sam."

Sam.

"According to Gary Chapman, quality time is the most common love language, followed by physical touch and words of affirmation for men. Words of affirmation would most likely apply to an insecure man. There are many of those in the world, trust me on this, and you do not fit in this category. Quality time would be a man who is conformable in close proximity to others, and places high value on the friendships and relationships in their lives—you do not."

"Incorrect. I value a few people. Would die for them, actually."

"Yeah, but you wouldn't cuddle up and watch a movie with them." When he shrugged, I continued. "Acts of service wouldn't fit you because you're obviously a solitary soul and a control freak. Lastly, receiving gifts—also not you. You can't even handle the emotion of a simple thank-you."

Roman frowned. "I'm not sure I like the picture of the man you painted."

I shrugged, mocking him. "You are physical touch, no doubt about it."

"What about you?" he asked, handing me the canteen.

I sipped, then swallowed. "What about me?"

"What's your . . . language, or whatever."

I sighed. "Unfortunately, words of affirmation."

"Why unfortunately?"

"Unfortunately because I've yet to meet a man with the emotional maturity to speak this love language to me."

Or love me at all in the first place.

"Emotions make you messy," he said.

"Emotions make a life worth living."

Roman stared at me for a minute, thinking.

Mercenaries didn't care about life or death—right?

He pulled another granola bar from the pack and handed it to me. A clever diversion from a conversation getting too deep for his comfort.

"One more," he said.

"Are you sure?"

"Yes."

"Thank you."

He dipped his chin.

I devoured the gooey oats, watching him. "Aren't you going to eat?"

"I had something while you slept."

Oh.

I shifted on the fern leaves, sitting straighter, feeling better. "Have you been able to communicate with whoever was supposed to take us to the airport? The guy who took out the man shooting at me while I escaped?"

"No. His name is Bear, and we lost contact after the chaos at the lodge."

"Is he someone you work with? At Astor Stone?"

"No. We served together in the military."

"Ah. Who is Astor Stone?"

"A sadistic, cunning businessman who would have me killed if he knew how sideways this op has gone."

"*Killed*?"

"Yes. Astor doesn't accept failure."

"Sounds like a horrible boss."

"He has singlehandedly built one of the most highly respected paramilitary companies in the country, under the guise of a private investigation firm. The DOD considers him invaluable to their international operations. He's efficient, structured, insanely smart, and puts the mission above all else. I respect him."

"You respect a man who would kill you?"

"For the greater good? Yes."

"Wow." I angled my head toward him. "How old are you?"

"Why? Does it matter?"

I wasn't sure why, but I detected a bit of insecurity in the question. As if he'd thought about our age difference already.

"No . . . I'm twenty-nine," I said, anxious for his reaction to this.

"I know."

"You know?"

"Yes."

"Ah, that's right, from your intel package on me."

"Right."

"So, how old are you?" I asked.

"Forty-two."

"You seem older."

"Thanks."

"I mean, in an experienced kind of way."

"Thanks." He rolled his eyes.

I grinned.

Roman regarded me closely. "You're an inquisitive creature, you know?"

"I ask a lot of questions. It's one of my worst qualities. I get it from my mom. She likes to know about people, to understand them and what makes them tick. This is why she was such a great teacher—and why I became one, for that matter. She . . ."

I stopped mid-sentence, feeling that damn knot rise in my throat.

"Emotions make you messy."

"I'm sorry for what you've been through," he said.

"Thank you, but I'm not the only one. I'm not the only victim. There are so many, Roman, so many innocent—"

"I know." His voice was suddenly sharp, a nerve within him struck.

A moment passed between us.

"How long have you been undercover?" I asked.

"A while."

"How long, Roman?"

"Thirty years."

"Thirty . . ." My jaw dropped. "Wait—so you would have been a child when you started working undercover. Why?"

Roman pulled the knife from his boot and began sharpening it against a rock. I got the sense it was a nervous tic.

"Why, Roman?" I pressed, wanting to know more about the man who attracted me in so many ways. "Why have you tethered your life to this horrible, vile world?"

"Because someone has to," he said, avoiding eye contact.

"There's a story here, isn't there? Please tell me."

No response.

I leaned forward, following my gut intuition. "Tell me about your mother. It's something to do with her, isn't it?"

His jaw twitched.

"I saw it in your eyes when I spoke of mine. When you

asked if my mom and I were close—I saw emotion in your eyes."

He sniffed dismissively, a bit of a snarl to his lip.

"Tell me," I said again quickly, before he could close up completely, knowing I was on to something.

A pair of ice-cold green eyes met mine.

"My mom is dead, Sam. She was murdered."

A piece of the complicated puzzle that was Roman Thieves clicked into place. His mother had been murdered, and somehow, in that moment, I knew this was his driving force. This was his life.

He refocused on sharpening the knife in his hand.

A long moment stretched between us as I tried to find the right words, but came up short.

Finally, he said quietly, "My mother was a victim of human trafficking."

My heart stuttered, my eyes widening.

"More than thirty years ago," he said, keeping his focus on the knife he was sharpening against the rock. "In Ireland, in the slums where I grew up. I was kidnapped when I was nine years old. They kept me chained like a dog in a house only three blocks from where I lived. After a few days, I was returned to my mother, on threat of death if she didn't do as they said. They used me as bait to make her work for them. Told her that they would kill me if she didn't work for them."

His strokes against the stone became more aggressive,

the grate of the blade against stone like nails on a chalkboard.

"This went on for three years. Random men in and out of our house. Taking me away for hours when she wouldn't comply or do exactly as they told her to do. And then I would be brought back—I know now because she finally complied . . . I know now that's why her eyes were so vacant every time they brought me back. They stole a little piece of my mother every time I was taken away."

The knife violently sliced at the rock.

"Until they eventually took all of her." A beam of sunlight reflected in his feral, deadly eyes. "And killed her and left her corpse to rot in a dirty alleyway."

A bright red streak of blood ran down his hand.

"Roman . . ." I pushed up and dropped to my knees in front of him. Frantic, I grabbed his wrist and squeezed, stopping the manic sharpening. "You're bleeding, Roman."

Carefully, I pried the knife from his vise-like grip and rolled over his wrist. Blood pulsed from a deep gash that ran from the top of his wrist to the pad of his thumb.

"*Jesus*, Roman."

The cut was deep. The bleeding wasn't stopping anytime soon.

I was astonished that he hadn't reacted when it happened. Hell, maybe he hadn't even noticed.

Roman was staring at the ground, his face flushed red, his breathing heavy—not with pain, but with anger. Mentally, he was somewhere else entirely.

"Roman." I set the knife on a pad of fern leaves beside us. "Roman, look at me. Please. Take a deep breath."

He turned to me but didn't focus.

"Take a deep breath."

His pupils dilated. His jaw unclenched.

"Inhale, exhale . . ."

Locking eyes with him, I watched the anger slide from his face like a melting candle. "That's it."

He blinked wildly as if just returning to the present moment, then squinted at the blood pooling in his palm. Still, no emotion. He stared at his hand as if trying to figure out how the blood had gotten there.

"It's a deep cut," I said. "Do you have a first aid kit in your pack?"

He frowned, yanking his hand away. "It's fine."

I pulled it back. "No, it isn't. It needs to be tended to."

"Sam, it's *fine*. It doesn't—"

He started to yank it away again, but I clamped down on his fingers like a bear trap.

"*Stop*, you stubborn hypocrite." I shook my head, examining the wound. "God, you're something else, you know that?" I angrily jerked his hand. "Be still."

I wiped away the blood with the bottom of my—his—T-shirt. The gash was deeper than I'd realized.

Keeping my grip on his wrist, I awkwardly stretched and grabbed the pack that was almost out of reach. I knew if I let him go, he'd be gone. The man wouldn't accept help on his deathbed.

I rummaged through the pack until I found a small bag that appeared to be a first aid kit. Using cotton balls and peroxide, I cleaned the wound.

"It needs stitches."

My heart skipped at the expression on his face.

He was fixed on me—not his wound—his stare so intense that butterflies exploded in my stomach. There was a hint of confusion in the crease of his brow. By my taking care of him? By his reaction to it?

Feeling my cheeks flush, I returned my focus to the

wound. I didn't know what the hell I was doing. I had no idea how to stitch someone up.

Well, there's a first time for everything.

Roman remained still and silent as I rummaged through the pack. No butterfly bandages, but I did find black duct tape and scissors.

I cut several short, thin strips of tape. One by one, I used them to close the wound.

Roman watched me—not his hand—the entire time.

My pulse rate had picked up somewhere during the application of the second strip. I could *feel* the sexual tension bouncing between us like an invisible force.

After securing the last piece, I cut a strip from one of the ACE bandages I wore as shoes and wrapped it around his palm.

"Don't use this hand for the rest of the day," I told him. "Seriously. The cut needs to close. I'm not a survivalist, but it's deep enough to worry about getting infected. Just," I sighed, "relax for a minute."

27

"*J*ust . . . *relax for a minute.*"

The last time I'd been told to relax, I was eleven years old. My mother was cooking breakfast. I'd demanded to help because I couldn't sit still. I kept waiting for the men to return, to take her away again. I knew she needed to rest because she always seemed so tired and sad when they returned her, though she tried to conceal it from me.

"*Relax, Roman, please, relax for a minute . . . You need to learn to just relax, my beautiful son.*"

She made chocolate chip cookies for me that day.

That was the last time a woman had ever done anything for me that didn't involve balancing on her knees. That was the last time someone had truly cared for me and my well-being. That someone had simply *helped* me.

It seems like such a simple thing, helping someone, and that someone accepts the help. Such an easy thing to do, but you'd be surprised by how many don't even think of it.

Because of losing my mother so young and in such a savage way, I'd developed a hard personality, a tough, callous outer shell that made people cross to the other side of the street when they saw me coming. A persona that implied not only that I, this big, tall, mean man, never needed help, but that I wouldn't have accepted it anyway.

And perhaps they were right . . . I wouldn't know. Because no one had ever tried. Until now.

This beautiful, strong, smart, damn stubborn woman wanted to help *me*. It felt . . . confusing. Comforting. Humbling.

Exhilarating, exciting.

Something sparked to life in me that day, a small flame somewhere in the depths of my polluted black soul.

A flame for her, for Samantha Greene, a reminder of the good in the world, of the purest soul.

A tiny light in the darkness.

28

I gently placed his hand in his lap, settled back onto the ground, and propped my elbows on my knees.

"What happened to you then?" I asked. "After they killed your mother in front of you?"

"I killed my first man."

"When you were twelve years old?"

"Yes. With a kitchen knife."

A withered brown leaf fluttered down from a nearby tree. We watched it a moment, lazily swaying on the wind.

"Do you regret it?" I asked.

"No."

"But it didn't satisfy you, did it? Killing the man didn't take it all away, did it?"

His eyes met mine, understanding flickering between us. He knew I'd spent hours planning how I would one day kill the men holding me captive.

Roman picked up a handful of soil, then slowly let it sift between his fingertips. "Two men killed my mother that night. I killed one, but the other got away."

"Who did you kill?"

"Oisin Cussane."

My eyes rounded.

"The one who got away was his son, Conor Cussane, who became the head of one of the largest human-trafficking organizations in the world, the man responsible for your abduction. The man I am—was—supposed to meet, for the first time ever, today at the lodge."

My eyes rounded as my brain struggled to catch up with this turn of events. "You mean to tell me that the son of the man who killed your mother is the same man who kidnapped me? The man I was supposed to be enslaved to and make babies with?"

"Yes."

Tick—the final piece of the puzzle clicked together.

"So, that's why you've made this your life mission. You're seeking revenge for your mother."

He said nothing. He didn't need to.

Roman had agreed to take my mission, to save me, only because it provided another opportunity to get close to the leader of the CUN.

I was nothing more than a means to an end.

And why the hell did this bother me so much?

"So, even though you killed the man who killed your mother, you're still going to kill Conor? An eye-for-an-eye type of thing?"

"I don't expect you to understand."

"I'd rethink that statement if I were you, Roman."

He looked up, seeing in my eyes what I'd been through. "I'm sorry."

I nodded, then continued. "So, you've been seeking revenge one way or another for her since you were twelve years old?" The thought was almost unfathomable.

"After I killed Oisin, I tried to forget everything. Figured justice was served. I lived on the streets until I was sixteen. Then I lived with a friend, a few years older, who had a house. I worked as a dishwasher during the days, ran drugs during the night, collecting intel here and there of the CUN. I was acting undercover before I even realized it."

He shook his head as if he'd just now understood that fact.

"It happened slowly, really. I made a few connections, then realized it was easier to make more connections if I were undercover. Eventually, I saved up enough money and got the next flight out of Ireland to America. I wanted to leave everything behind. Try to start a new life. Turns out, a change of scenery doesn't take the pain away."

"Did you ever go back?"

"Home?"

"Yeah."

"No." Roman plucked a stone from the ground and tossed it into the jungle. "Our neighbor, her name is Freya, cleaned out our house after the eviction notices began piling up." He snorted out a pathetic laugh. "The woman has made it her damn life mission to send me my mom's things."

"That must be hard, seeing her things again."

"I wouldn't know. I've never accepted them back. After I moved away, Freya contacted a friend of mine named Kieran Healy, who gave her my personal email address. She keeps emailing me, asking where I want her to send everything. I've never responded."

"Roman—"

"I know, I know."

"No, seriously. This could be a huge part of the closure I think you need so badly. Let her send you everything. I'll bet it will help." I put my hand on his knee. "There's got to be a point where you just have to accept that it happened and let it all go, Roman. Hang on to the good memories, but let the pain go."

He seemed to contemplate this, then said, "My mom was super religious. Funny, huh?"

"Why funny?"

"Well, I don't understand why she let it go on. Why she allowed the men to control her life . . . Why she allowed all this evil into her life if she claimed to believe in God and heaven and all that stuff. She never even called the cops, you know. Never once. I don't understand it."

"She did it for you."

He shook his head.

"Roman, she did it to protect you."

Pain squeezed his face. "I don't think she would approve of me now."

"I think you're using that as a way out."

Frowning, he glared at me.

"I mean, you feel like you're already past the point of saving. She wouldn't approve, so you might as well keep crossing the line between good and evil, right? It's a lot easier to keep doing something you know you're not supposed to, than to make the effort to stop and turn it around."

"I've done *a lot* of things I'm not supposed to, Sam."

"So, turn it around."

We watched a duo of birds flutter from bush to bush in front of us, blazing yellows and reds, a few minutes of silence passing as we contemplated the things we're not supposed to do.

"So, you just came to America with nothing?" I asked.

"Yep. Not even a single suitcase. I got my green card,

enlisted in the Navy. Was eventually promoted into special ops. This is when I learned Oisin's son, Conor, had taken up his father's sword, so to speak, and was slowly growing the Cussane Network into a global business. And just like that, I was back in the game, reaching out to old drug connections back in Ireland, gathering intel, sliding back into that world. I became obsessed all over again."

Roman stared at his hands, his eyes unfocused.

"This was when Astor recruited me. I was twenty-one and have worked for him ever since. Then I quickly realized that working for Astor gave me access to endless resources, so much information, and that's when my search really picked up steam. I began using my missions to investigate the Cussane Network on my own, to track the son of the man who killed my mother."

He was lost in thought for moment.

"Then on a mission in Mexico, I stumbled onto an opportunity to participate in a sale—"

"Of humans?"

"Yes. I bought a girl that day." There was a hint of shame in his eyes. "I paid a lot of money for her. Then I bought another, and another, and I realized the amount I spent on the girls started giving me notoriety. I wore black suits to every sale, fully immersing myself into this character I'd created. This is when I met Lucas Ruiz, an undercover agent for the Mexican government. He'd lost his sister and two cousins to the sex trade. We began sharing information—bonded, you could say—and we've worked together ever since."

"What did you do with the girls? After you bought them?"

"I sent them to a rehabilitation shelter in the US."

"And how are they now? The girls?"

Roman shrugged.

My brows popped. "You don't know?"

"No."

"You never followed up?"

"No."

"You saved these girl's lives, and you're not the least bit curious how their lives turned out?"

"No."

"I don't believe you."

"I don't care."

"You just don't want to get involved past *the mission*. It's too emotional for you."

"You're too emotional for me."

I rolled my eyes. "Seriously, Roman, I'm sure they'd love to see you. To thank you. And whether you realize it or not, I'm sure you would get some sort of closure from seeing the good work that you did."

He shrugged again.

"Does Astor know that you've been using his company to advance your own personal vendetta?"

"I think he has an idea. My connections in the human-trafficking community are no secret—which is why I was hand-selected for your mission. But no one knows why, about my mom, and exactly how deep my connections run. He's never asked—and my ulterior motives have never ruined one of my ops or affected them negatively. I've done my jobs to the best of my ability, and that's all that matters to Astor. This is a side thing I do."

A moment passed.

"I want to help," I said.

He frowned at me. "Help what?"

"I want you to get revenge for your mother. And I want to get those goddamn kids out of there, Roman. Do you realize they're about the same age you were when you killed your first man? Do you want them to turn out as jaded and hard as you?"

Roman stilled, the words hitting him hard.

"Get your revenge and let's get the kids home. Roman, *please.*"

"You only feel guilty because you were saved and they weren't."

"That's not all it is. You should have seen their faces . . . the fear. I can't imagine—"

"*Stop*," he hissed, holding up his palm, his focus suddenly snapping to the trees in front of us.

"What?" I whispered, every muscle in my body going rigid.

"Stay still—we aren't alone."

29

SAM

*C*haos erupted before I even knew what was happening.

Roman flattened on the ground, surged onto his feet, and lunged into the trees before I could form a single thought. I scrambled up, slipping on the loose soil as I lurched forward, away from whatever—or whoever—Roman was attacking in the woods.

I lunged into the shadows, jumped behind a tree, and gaped at the man.

Capitán.

Pinned underneath Roman was the one-eyed man who'd kept me captive for months. The monster who'd clipped the brunette's finger, days after clipping my own. Once I realized this, my instinct then wasn't to flee, but to help Roman beat the man to death.

Except he wasn't beating him—and the man wasn't fighting him, either.

Flummoxed, I watched Roman stand, reach out his hand, and pull Capitán off the ground. He dusted himself off, and they began speaking in Spanish.

There was no thinking, no hesitation on my part.

I pulled the knife Roman had given me and lunged forward with a guttural scream.

If Roman hadn't tackled me to the ground, I would have killed the man, right there in the middle of the jungle. There is no question in my mind.

"Sam, *stop!*" Straddling me, Roman jerked the knife from my grasp and pinned my wrists above my head.

"Kill him!" I screamed like a wild animal. "*Kill him*, Roman!"

"Sam, *stop.*" His grip around my wrists tightened as I writhed underneath him. "Look at me . . . Sam, look at me. Calm down, look at me, look at me."

I blinked, focusing on the words, on him. On his eyes.

"That's right," he said softly. "Take a deep breath. Calm down. I'm here, right here. Inhale, exhale. *Breathe*, Sam."

I did, stilling underneath him, our eyes locked with the unspoken trust that had already been formed between us.

"This is Lucas Ruiz," he told me. "He's with the Mexican government. He's the undercover agent I was just telling you about."

"He's—*what*?"

"That's right. He's undercover like I am."

"But, Roman, he's . . . the things he's done . . ."

"I know, Sam." Roman inhaled deeply, guilt marring his own face. "I know."

It was then, for the first time, that I wondered about all the things Roman had done while undercover. A sick feeling knotted my stomach.

When Roman released me, I shot to my feet and stared at the man, Lucas Ruiz.

"But he—*you* . . ." I sneered at Lucas. "Those children—"

"It's part of it, Sam." Roman interrupted, opening his palms like there was nothing he could do about it.

"Bullshit," I snapped. "It's fucked up."

"I know—but it's the only way to infiltrate and stop a group like this. It's part of the job." Roman stepped between Lucas and me, blocking my view of the man. He gripped my shoulders, his stare penetrating. "Sam, you have to trust m—"

"I do."

Roman dipped his chin, released me, and turned to Lucas, the two quickly falling into hushed conversation.

I do trust you, I thought as I stared at the men before me. *I trust him, I trust him, I trust him.*

Cautiously, I stepped forward, careful to stay behind Roman and keep my distance from the man who'd kept me locked in a cage for weeks.

I hated him. Regardless of what appeared to be a working relationship between my savior and my captor, I hated the man with one eye.

Lucas spoke quickly. "I only have a few minutes," he said in English.

I pitifully laughed to myself. I'd assumed he could only speak Spanish.

"How far off are they?" Roman asked.

"Six miles southeast. Your man, Bear, diverted them to the river by laying tracks. They're still following the tracks, thinking they belong to her. I volunteered to venture off path, knowing your escape route."

Roman had shared his escape route with Lucas before shit went down, apparently. I couldn't process it all. It felt so wrong.

Lucas continued. "They're getting restless. Panicking.

Conor still hasn't showed, and now one of the slaves is missing and two of their men are dead."

"Four."

"Not according to them. They never found the bodies you dragged to the shed. I dumped them in a nearby river before they could find them. There was no way to explain the gunshots—they would know someone was watching. As far as I can tell, the guards think those two men went into town on break."

"What about the bodies in the room?"

There was a flash of disapproval on Lucas's face before he continued. "They suspect the girl did it and they want her head. I slit their throats with a butter knife from the kitchen, then marred the bedpost to make it look like she'd somehow gotten ahold of a knife, got herself loose, and jumped the men. They think you went off after her, to try to find her."

"So, Roman's cover is still intact?" I asked.

"Right now, yes. But not if he doesn't return with your head soon enough."

"Christ." Roman ran his fingers through his hair. "How long do we have until they wise up and send an entire army after us?"

"Not long. I'm due back in a few hours. When I tell them I've come up emptyhanded, they'll send more out." He paused. "And . . . you know I'm leaving today. I won't be around to help you any more come this afternoon."

"Your daughter?"

"Yes. She's very close to labor now. I leave before sundown."

Roman glanced at me.

"You need to get out of here," Lucas said. "Get to the

airport as soon as possible . . ." He scowled at me. "What's your ETA?"

How much is she slowing you down, he meant.

"Three days."

"Three days? Shit, man. Can't your buddy Bear help get her there faster?"

"We lost contact after the gunfire."

Lucas shook his head. "My men are following his tracks. They'll find him, you know. Then you'll have no one."

"No, they won't. Bear is smart. He's diverting them from me intentionally. He knows what he's doing. Trust me. This is what he does."

"Well, let's hope you're right." Lucas shook out of his backpack, unzipped it, and handed Roman a small bag that was tucked inside. "Food, water, medical supplies, a lighter. It was all I could scrounge up at the last minute."

"Thanks." Roman stuffed the provisions into his pack.

"Get out of here, Roman," Lucas said, backing into the shadows. "Now."

And like a ghost, he was gone.

30

SAM

*R*oman and I quickly packed up and switched direction, him leading me away from the path we'd been trekking since the escape. Being overly cautious, I assumed.

The run-in with Lucas had sobered us both, reignited a fear inside me.

"They want her head."

The temperature had climbed to what I could only imagine was triple digits. We hiked up mountains, down mountains, through valleys, tepid streams, under fallen logs, over fallen logs. I'd never been more thankful for trees in my life. Without the shade they provided, I'm sure I would have died of a heat stroke.

We didn't stop the rest of that day. Only brief pauses of Roman forcing me to drink and eat—ignoring my insistence that he do the same—and him checking my wrapped feet.

Roman was resolute, more determined than ever to complete the first phase of his mission—returning me home safely. Failure wasn't an option. Not because he cared about me, I told myself, but because he had phase two to complete after. A very personal, very deadly final mission that ended with the death of the son of the man who'd killed Roman's mother.

I was nothing but a task to complete, a burden to, quite literally, offload.

I spent the day brooding over and dissecting this very thought. Eventually, I came up with three reasons for my fragile feelings about the situation.

One, I was sick of being treated like nothing more than an object. Something to mold, to sell, to use, to deliver from point A to point B. It was as if the world had simply removed my identity. I was nothing more than a hollow shell, unworthy of proper attention and, dare I say, care. I was a package being delivered. That was it.

Two, I couldn't stop thinking about the children we'd left behind. Guilt consumed me, randomly mixing with anger at the fact that Roman seemed so unsympathetic to them. But what did I expect? *I* was the mission. They weren't. Roman only cared about me because that was his only commitment. Get me from point A to point B, then refocus on his real mission.

And finally, I realized that Roman's seemingly objectification of me bothered me because I was absolutely enraptured by the man. Despite everything, he had ignited feelings that confused, exhausted, and disoriented me. And at the same time made me feel giddy and gave me *all* the butterflies.

Damn him. Damn him, *damn him.*

I was near death (felt like, anyway) by the time the sun finally slipped behind the treetops. This, I'd learned, was the worst time for bugs.

We stopped at the edge of a creek where tall, mature

trees formed a tunnel around it. The waning light dappled the water like little round mirrors floating on the current.

Roman slipped out of his pack.

Do we sit? Are you allowing me to sit?

I lingered behind him as he pulled out what appeared to be a small polished stick from the bag, then proceeded to expand it like a selfie tripod (this description punctuating the difference in our lifestyles). When I saw the string, I realized the stick wasn't a stick at all—it was a portable fishing rod.

Next, Roman toe-heeled out of his boots and began unbuttoning his pants.

"What are you doing?" I asked, my heart rate picking up considerably.

"Fishing."

I glanced at the creek, at the rotted old log stretching from one side to the other, the boulders spearing up from the murky blackness, the grassy overhangs that surely lent themselves to a den of snakes. It was nothing like the serene rivers and lakes my father and I had fished when I was a little girl.

"You're fishing in *there*?" I asked.

"Are you hungry?"

I licked my lips. I was absolutely starving.

Reluctantly, I nodded.

"Then yes," he said simply. "I'm fishing in there."

His pants fell to his feet, revealing a tight pair of black boxer briefs.

And since when did I have a leg fetish?

Roman's thighs were as thick as tree trunks, his calves carved to perfection. His ass was like two bowling balls, and his bulge—dear Lord in Heaven . . .

The shirt came off next.

Was I hungry? Uh, yeah . . . but for something entirely different from food now.

Obviously comfortable and unaffected by stripping in front of a woman, Roman grabbed his rod—the wooden one, to my dismay—and strode half-naked into the water.

I shifted my weight, feeling useless, standing there in my baggy T-shirt and tactical pants, with my dirty, wrapped feet. I watched him pick a spot, widen his stance, and settle in.

Suddenly, he stilled, and a beam of light darted across his face.

My stomach tickled.

"Come here," he said, but I didn't move. "Come here."

"Uh . . . there?"

"Yes. Here."

"Okay." I lowered down, unwrapped my feet, and literally exhaled when they were freed. The fresh air felt like cool silk over the throbbing, hot, swollen skin.

My cheeks heated as I unbuttoned my pants, and I mentally laughed at this. The man had already seen me stark naked, chained to a bed.

I glanced up, peeking at him under my lashes. He was watching me intently, and suddenly, the moment felt more like an erotic strip tease rather than two people trying to survive in the wild.

I slipped out of the pants, taking the time to fold them neatly, and set them aside while trying to conjure up some courage. Luckily, the oversized T-shirt covered all my bits, the bottom seam hitting just below the crease of my butt.

In nothing but the shirt, I tiptoed my way over the sharp rocks and waded into the water.

"Hooooly . . ." I squealed with delight as the cold water slipped between my toes. If heaven had a feeling, this was it.

Carefully, slowly, I made my way over the slick rocks to

Roman in the middle of the stream. The water hit me midthigh, cooling my legs.

"Fish have four basic needs, just like we do," he said as I approached.

For some reason, I was disappointed. In my fantasy, I imagined him so attracted to me that seeing me in nothing but his T-shirt would render him incapable of control, and he would toss me over his shoulder, carry me to a bed of ferns, spread my—

"They need oxygen, food, shelter, and rest," he said, jerking me from my fantasy. "The best time to catch a fish is when they're fulfilling need number two, food."

I nodded as I stared at the water, pretending I wasn't totally clueless.

"Tell me what you see around us."

I frowned. "You mean . . . like . . .

"Just tell me what you see. Look around. Take it in."

"Okay . . . I see beautiful white flowers on the shoreline."

"Those are plumeria trees. They're all over. White, pink, orange. You're familiar with Hawaiian leis?"

I nodded.

"Those are the flowers used to make them. Stunning, aren't they?"

I smirked.

"What?"

"Nothing."

"What?"

"Stunning isn't a word I expected from you in casual conversation . . . or *beautiful* for that matter."

He regarded me closely. Intimately. "I call it like I see it, Samantha."

I tucked a strand of hair behind my ear while blushing

like a schoolgirl. *Damn this man and his ability to turn me into a puddle of stupidity.*

"What else do you see?" he said, returning to the subject.

"I see rocks and rushing water." I followed the whitecaps. "I see a large boulder over there." I pointed ahead. "A fallen log and more rocks past that."

"Right. Exactly. Good job. There are five sections of a river. We're standing in what's called the riffle—shallow and rocky with surface movement." Roman motioned a few feet ahead where the water moved smoothly with the current. "That's called a run, and to the right of the boulder over there is a pool of deep, calm water. Just past the boulder is called an eddy—this is where the current is disturbed, in this case by the boulder it swirls around. Past the pool and eddy is the tailout, where it gets shallower. Tell me, where do you think is the best place to catch a fish?"

I had absolutely no idea.

"Think, Sam. Tap into your survival instinct."

I took a deep breath and pointed to the pool. "There, where it's deep, so they can hide."

"Incorrect."

Dammit.

"Remember, we're fishing with bait, which means we want the fish who are looking for food. See the eddy?"

I squinted, trailing the swirling water with my eyes, seeing tiny specks caught in the current. Bugs—food.

My eyes rounded.

Smiling, he nodded. "That's right. Those insects are caught in the swirl of the current, therefore attracting fish. There is where we want to focus."

When a fin suddenly flicked out of the water, I gasped, pointing. "Did you see that?"

He winked. "Yep. Dinner."

The lesson continued with Roman showing me how to —*correctly*—use a fishing rod, how to bait, then cast.

How to wait.

Wait . . .

And freaking *wait*.

Night came hard and quick, like a veil of blackness descending on the jungle.

My legs were weak from balancing on the slick rocks, my body tired, impatient.

Suddenly, the rod jerked. In one fluid movement, Roman yanked the line from the water. A spinning, flipping fish hung from the line.

I screamed with delight.

"Stay here," he said, his tone excited, childlike. "They're biting. Hang on."

Roman jogged to shore, unhooked the fish, and secured it in a bag. He jogged back, water splashing around his ankles. The excitement between us was palpable, and I realized then that he must be starving too—and then I realized that I hadn't seen him eat once that day. Not a single time.

Had he? Or was he reserving all the food for me?

We caught three more fish in under twenty minutes, then waded back to shore.

Roman built a fire at the base of two large boulders covered in vibrant green moss, the massive structures hiding the flames from anyone who might be lurking in the shadows. He'd pulled on his pants, leaving his glorious bare chest on full display. He also had beautiful feet, and a little part of me hated him for that. I had bunions.

The man was perfect . . . except for the whole hired-gun thing.

I opted out of the lesson on skinning, instead pretending

to take rest against the rock while secretly drooling over the view of his bare chest.

An hour later, we ate like starving POWs next to the fire, under the stars.

My body temperature had cooled, my belly was full, and for the first time since I was captured, I peered up at the sky and felt content. I felt free, happy . . . and then felt him staring at me.

Our eyes met, and I smiled.

Something flickered in his eyes, the electricity between us sparking hot.

I became aware of my body, the reaction he was giving me, and was reminded of how pitiful I must seem. I examined the dirt-ridden clothes I wore, my knobby knees, the cut and bruised ankles.

God, how I'd kill for a—

A bar of soap landed in my lap.

My eyes rounded and my jaw dropped as I picked up the bar and gaped at Roman.

His lips twitched, fighting a smile.

"Oh my G—*soap*?"

He nodded.

"Oh my *God*. You've had this the whole freaking time?" I surged to my feet. "I haven't bathed in—"

Shut up, Samantha, shut up.

"Sorry," he said, "I didn't think about it."

"About *bathing*? You didn't think about *bathing*?"

He shook his head, a glint of amusement in his eyes. "I'm in survival mode right now. The longest I've gone without bathing on a mission is sixteen days."

I jerked back, gasping in horror.

He laughed. "Remember the pool, next to the eddy? Should be deep enough to dip under the water there."

"The pool . . ." I squinted in that direction, trying to make out the stream through the blackness. "Isn't that kind of far? How far is it from here?"

"A few yards."

I rolled my eyes. "How far in woman terms?"

"About a three-minute walk."

I stared into the black night.

"Are you afraid one of the ghosts that haunt these mountains is going to get you?" he asked, mocking me.

I fisted a hand on my hip. "I don't believe in ghosts in that way. I believe in spirits. People with unfinished business."

"Okay, are you afraid someone with unfinished business is going to get you?"

"You're an ass. And it's not that."

"I won't look," he said, picking up on my hesitation.

"No, it's not that either."

I'm scared to leave you.

As if reading my thoughts, Roman pushed off the ground, dusted off his pants, and crossed the rocks. "Come on." He took my hand.

I bowed my head as he led me through the darkness, allowing him to guide me, to take care of me. Oh God, how I loved that feeling. Even just pretending for a moment that he cared, that someone *wanted* to take care of me.

We stopped at the edge of the water. He made a show of turning his back to me, then gestured for me to get on with it.

"Undress?" I asked, my voice cracking with nerves.

"I'm not sure how you're going to bathe with your clothes on."

Good point.

I stood paralyzed with fear like a pre-teen in the locker

room.

"I'm not going to look," he said impatiently.

I don't know why the hell I was so nervous.

Because you like him, Sam. You want him to think you're pretty.

All of a sudden, Roman sighed mockingly and began unbuttoning his pants.

"What the hell are you doing?" I squeaked.

"Getting naked so you won't be so damn nervous."

"You think *you* getting naked is going to make me *less* nervous?"

"Yeah. Isn't that how it works?" His pants fell to the ground.

"Yep." I nodded. "That's exactly how it works—in *prison*."

He slipped out of his boxers and turned to me.

I slapped my hands over my eyes like an idiot. "J—just turn around. *Jesus*, Roman."

"What?" He chuckled. "See? Now we're both naked."

I heard the *flop*, *flop*, *flop* of balls against thighs as he playfully wiggled his midsection, followed by a full-blown laugh.

Another dramatic eye roll (from under the palm of my hand). "Are you sure you're forty-two?"

"Yep, and *all* man." Another *flop, flop.*

"God, you're so—"

"Helpful?"

"No." I sighed and shook my head. "Just turn around."

Still chuckling, he turned.

Keeping one eye on his ass cheeks—which were glorious, by the way—I quickly stripped, pulling the T-shirt over my head and tossing it onto the ground.

"Keep turned around until I get to the water," I said.

"Is this really necessary, Sam?"

"Yes."

I darted across the rocks on my tiptoes and splashed into the water.

I exhaled, relishing the coolness washing over my skin. The water was the perfect temperature, not too warm, not too cold.

I felt a rush of happiness, a childlike joy as I threw myself into the water.

"You good?" he yelled over the splashing.

"*Yes*." I squatted down, slipped to my butt—hiding all my bits—and splashed the water onto my face, feeling like a kid at the city pool on summer break. "Bring me the soap."

I turned away as he waded into the water, offering him privacy that he didn't demand.

"The pool is over here," he said, extending his palm.

My hand slid into his. Keeping his eyes respectfully forward, Roman led me to the middle of the stream.

Goose bumps rippled over my skin as the water slowly rose up my body. The contrast of the cool water and the heat from his touch ignited every sexual sensor in my body. It was erotic, him guiding me naked down the stream, the moon lighting our way. It felt like primitive times, a man taking care of his woman. Guiding her, teaching her, protecting her.

And if I'm being honest, it was sexy as shit.

"There's a drop-off a few feet ahead," he said, "but you should be able to touch. I'll wait here."

This time I didn't ask him to close his eyes. I banished my nerves, pulled my shoulders back, lifted my chin, and waded into the water ahead. The drop-off was sudden, and I allowed myself to fall, letting go. I dipped under the water and spun around, a smile on my face. I emerged like Ariel, sans the shell bikini top and abnormally perfect breasts.

Our eyes met.

Roman smiled, but this smile was different from the ones before. This smile gave me butterflies.

Wading, I tested the bottom with my feet. Once I was certain I could touch, I settled in, the water hitting just below my collarbone.

"Soap." I held out my hand.

Roman nodded to a large rock at the drop-off. He'd already tossed it to me while I was pretending to be a mermaid. I swam over, grabbed the soap, paused, and glanced over my shoulder.

He smirked, shook his head, and turned around.

I pulled myself onto the rock and began vigorously scrubbing my body, washing away the stink and slime from the men who'd held me captive. Washing away the dirt, the blood, the flashbacks, the memories.

I imagined clumps of the last two weeks dropping off my body, slowly disappearing into the black water below. I scrubbed my hair, my face, inhaling the fresh scent, smiling like an idiot. Finally, I dipped under, like a bird in a bird-bath, happy for the first time in weeks. Feeling like I was shedding all the bad things that had happened to me.

When I resurfaced, Roman had turned and was watching me.

He was nothing but a black silhouette now, a large, looming presence. One that made me feel 100 percent safe.

We stared at each other a long moment.

"Come in," I whispered, but he hesitated. "Come in."

He moved slowly, wading across the shallows, then dipped into the water, slipping off the edge and into the pool.

He kept his distance.

Holding up the soap, I slowly swam over to him. My

heart began to pound.

Roman stood strong and rigid as I approached. I stopped inches in front of him.

His eyes were intense with thought. Something was on his mind.

"How did you know Ardri translated to *high king* in Gaelic?" he asked softly.

I frowned, tracing memories back to the cave after he'd saved me. "Oh. I remember it from a fairy tale . . . one that my mom would read to me when I was a little girl."

"Tell me about it."

"Well . . ." I ran my fingers through my wet hair, fidgeting with the bottom strands. "It was stereotypical European folklore, the knight saving the damsel in distress. The princess, the dragon, the whole thing. I had a crush on the hero for years. Literally."

"Because he saved her."

"I guess so."

Roman reached forward, took the strand of hair I was fidgeting with, and gently placed it behind my shoulder. "What if the hero was also the villain?" he whispered, stepping closer.

"You're not bad, Roman," I whispered back.

"Yes, I am. Answer my question. What if the hero was also the villain? What if he is imperfect?"

I lifted my deformed hand. "So am I."

He wrapped his hands around my hand and kissed the nub where my pinky finger should have been.

I placed my other hand on his chest, leaning in. "Maybe in this fairy tale, we could find a way to save each other."

Something in his eyes flashed.

"Roman, I—"

"May I kiss you?" he whispered, almost breathlessly.

"*Yes.*"

My heart thundered as he gently wrapped his hands around my face, leaned down, and kissed me under the moonlight.

An explosion of fireworks danced in my body.

I threw my arms around his neck. He pulled me in and our kisses turned heated, more frantic, wildly sexy. I released my weight and lifted off my feet, allowing the water to support me, like floating through a dream.

When I wrapped my legs around his waist, I felt his erection against the bottom of my ass. Moaning, he pulled back, then hugged me so tightly, his body trembled against mine.

Despite the intensity in his grasp, there was a feeling of letting go. Finally, both him and me, together.

Tears filled my eyes as I was overcome with a sudden rush of emotions.

I pulled back, dragging my fingers through his wet hair as we stared at each other, knowing everything had just changed.

His green eyes twinkled in the moonlight, a fearful desperation written on his face.

"I'm not good at this, Sam. *I'm* not good," he whispered, his voice trembling with emotion. "I don't do relationships. I'm going to fail at this. I—"

"*Shhh,*" I whispered back, trailing my thumb over his bottom lip. "Then I'll help you."

Something flashed in his eyes. He blinked, seemingly stunned at the words. I'd triggered something in him, and it was obvious he didn't quite know how to handle it. I could practically see his brain short-circuiting.

I smiled, unwrapped my legs from his waist, placed my hands on his chest, and took a step back.

"Enough for today," I whispered. "Let's get some sleep."

31

SAM

*H*olding my hand, Roman led me off the shoreline and into the jungle, retracing our steps back to the our campsite.

Suddenly, he stopped, his entire body freezing in place.

Fear sparked through my veins. "Roman—"

Pop!

A thousand pieces of bark exploded inches above my head.

Before my brain could even register that we were being shot at, Roman spun on his heel and lunged toward me, throwing his body over mine, guiding our fall into a thick bush of ferns. Instead of taking cover there, he gripped my shoulders and dragged me like a rag doll across the ground, shuffling backward on his knees.

More muted pops, more debris exploding everywhere. Leaves rained down on us.

"Stay down," he hissed. "Pull your knees to your chest in the fetal position."

Though his tone was razor sharp, his voice was calm and

controlled. This calmed me. I felt protected, despite knowing we were currently under attack.

I did as I was told, finding myself cocooned in the thick, gnarled roots of a massive tree.

More shots pinged off the branches around us.

Roman laid his body over mine as a shield. "*Shhh . . .*"

My chest heaving, I clamped my mouth shut and breathed through my nose in a feeble attempt to control the adrenaline surging through my body.

Suddenly, *thump, thump, thump.* The sound of approaching footsteps beat in time with my pounding heart. My eyes widened as panic engulfed me.

Roman glanced at me, again mouthing *shhh.*

The boots stopped on the opposite side of the tree. I could hear the heaving breaths and rustle of fabric as whoever was trying to kill us shifted his weight.

Had he assumed we'd been shot?

I blinked wildly, peering past Roman's body that covered me. Moonlight cut through the canopy. Shadows danced along the trees like ghosts coming for us.

Did I see someone else? Was there another shooter? Were we being flanked?

I was sure I was about to have a full-blown heart attack.

Roman, on the other hand, was like a statue, barely even breathing, it seemed.

Suddenly, everything went still.

The man, the breeze, the screaming bugs, the entire world around us.

Click.

I felt the slightest movement from Roman as he repositioned his foot.

Fear wrapped around my throat like a vise as I listened to the man slowly peering around the tree.

Roman lunged off my body, the swoosh of a knife being pulled from his boot in time with the lightning-quick speed of his attack.

I scrambled backward as Roman barreled into the shooter headfirst, shoving the knife in the man's stomach.

The moonlight caught the man's face the moment the blade severed his internal organs. Black eyes locked on mine in surprise. Fear. Sadness.

I recognized him as one of the guards.

I gasped, propelling myself backward, falling over the tree roots, and covered my ears as Roman violently pumped the knife in and out of the man, the sickening suction sound curdling my stomach.

Roman was an animal. Vicious.

It was shocking, jarring, right to my soul.

The man slumped over Roman's shoulder, his glassy eyes still on mine. Roman straightened, allowing the man's body to slip off his. The guard landed with a hard thud on the ground.

I stared at the back of Roman's silhouette, his head hung low, his hunched shoulders rising and falling heavily with adrenaline, blood dripping from the knife in his blood-covered hand.

Nerves cut through the curdling in my stomach.

He turned, and our eyes locked. Then he stared at the man for a moment.

My pulse roared as I stared at him, and for a moment, I imagined him kneeling down, decapitating and mutilating the dead body, because what he'd done simply wasn't enough.

There was a side to Roman that was absolutely terrifying. In that moment, I wondered how much of this savage, barbarous side of him would forever remain in his soul.

He wiped the knife against his pants, cleaning the blade and smearing more blood on himself. Blood that wasn't his own.

With the knife in his grasp, Roman returned to me silently and resumed his position of protection.

We lay there for hours between the roots, unmoving, silent, until finally, Roman deemed it safe to rise from our hiding spot.

There were no words spoken as he wrapped me into his arms, cradled me like a baby, and carried me back to our campsite.

No words as he laid me down, wrapped me in his arms, and pulled me tight against him.

Finally, I fell asleep.

32

SAM

I awoke the next morning wrapped in Roman's arms.

The leaves swayed above us on a gentle breeze. It was the time of early morning when the sun hadn't fully risen, subtly illuminating the jungle in a dim blue light. Life crackled around us in the trees, on the branches, on the ground, in the water nearby.

Life crackled between us.

Us.

The kiss.

Memories flooded me. The gunshots, the brutal slaying of the man who tried to kill us. Roman shielding me, protecting me. The kiss.

"I'm not good at this, Sam."

I sat up, a mixture of both excitement and terror rushing through my veins.

Does he regret it?

The thought churned my stomach. Because I, without question, did not regret the kiss.

I stared into the ferns, in the direction of what would

eventually be an airport that would take me home. Home—
and away from him.

It was our last day together, our last night.

God, how things had changed between us.

Fingertips softly swept over my lower back, goose
bumps following immediately after. I turned, peering down
into those deliciously gorgeous green eyes, puffy and
swollen with sleep.

It was the first time I'd seen him sleep.

A smile tugged at the corner of his lips.

We stared at each other a minute, gauging the climate
between us, both questioning the other.

"Are you okay?" I asked.

"Yes." His response was immediate and certain. "Are you
okay?"

I smiled. "Yes."

He pulled me down and wrapped me in his arms, and
with those few, simple words, the relationship between us
was solidified.

I felt both excitement and absolute terror.

Of all the men I could be falling in love with, I,
Samantha Greene, was falling in love with a mercenary.

After coffee and an MRE, Roman left me to pack up
while he did a perimeter check, ensuring no more guards
lurked in the shadows.

We started out before daybreak, neither of us acknowl-
edging the savage way Roman had killed the guard the night
before, or that it was our last day together.

We hiked all day. The morning was filled with casual
conversation, flirty banter, and a few stolen kisses here and
there.

We talked about anything and everything that morning,
aside from the fact that we would be leaving each other in

several hours. Roman led most of the conversations, uncharacteristically talking nonstop. It was as if his armor had been left in the stream after the kiss.

He taught me how to read the sun, how to start a fire with rocks. I learned that Roman was an only child, that he hates peanut butter, and has a blurred cartoonish tattoo of his childhood idol, Conan the Barbarian, tattooed on his thigh. This, a souvenir given to him for free by a stripper on a drunken night in Brazil. I didn't ask what he gave her to initiate the trade.

I learned that Roman pushes up his shirtsleeve when he becomes uncomfortable with the topic of conversation or is ready to change the subject. I learned that his eyes twinkle when he teaches survival tactics, and that he sneaks glances at my lips when I pretend to listen.

The afternoon, however, was filled with silence. The closer we got to civilization, the greater the weight that came with it.

I was going home to my mother, my job, my dog, my mind-numbingly boring life. And Roman was going back to his dangerous life as a hired gun. To where? I didn't know. For how long? I didn't know.

Most importantly . . . would we see each other again?

The thought that I might never look into those green eyes again, feel the way he made me feel, absolutely sickened me.

I observed him as we hiked through the woods. Wanting him to address it, to tell me he wanted to see me again. Tell me he loved me.

But Roman never once looked in my direction. Not a single time. Over the course of the afternoon, he'd closed up, closed himself off to me.

This would be it. I was sure of it.

It was fucked up.

I should have been elated that I was going home, that I'd been rescued from hell on earth. Instead, I was absolutely torn apart at the thought that my time with this man was ending. It felt like a little piece of my heart was being ripped from my chest with each mile we walked that day.

We passed a trio of hikers, the first we'd seen since escaping the lodge. Normal people, on vacation, escaping the stresses of work and family. While we, on the other hand, were running for our lives, leaving a handful of dead bodies in our wake. The hikers were clueless of this, of course, offering polite nods and greetings as we passed.

I thought of my friends back home.

How would our interactions change? What would they say? How would they treat me?

No one would ever understand what I'd been through. No one but Roman.

Would I ever be the same again?

Would I ever be normal again?

33

"Tell me about your mom," Roman said as we paused under a shade tree on an overlook, high above a sparkling blue river below. A magnificent waterfall poured down the opposite side of the ravine. We sat on the edge of the cliff, our legs dangling off.

"My mom is an angel on earth. She's dedicated her entire life to helping others. She's the most selfless person I've ever met."

Roman handed me a granola bar. I took it, although my stomach had soured.

"You want to know what's crazy?" I asked.

"Yes."

"Knowing the pain she's in right now has been the worst part of this entire thing. She's not in great health, you know. I hate that I'm contributing to that. Every day, I think about what I would do if something happened to her while I was in captivity. What if I wasn't there if, God forbid . . ." My jaw clenched with a rush of anger. "God, I hate them, Roman. I *hate* them."

"I know." He slid his hand over mine. "I understand."

I slowly nodded. He did understand, truly—possibly the only person on earth who did.

"Tell me about your mom," I said. "What was she like?"

Roman picked up a stone and tossed it in the air. We watched it slowly fall to the water below.

"She liked to bake," he said. "She made these banana-chocolate-chip pancakes every Sunday morning."

When I smiled, he continued.

"I don't know where she got the extra money, but every Sunday morning, I woke up to these pancakes." He laughed softly. "I'd look forward to it all week. Not just because they were the best ever—seriously, they were incredible—but because it was the only time of the week that she would sit with me, eat with me, and eat until her belly was full. It was the only time she would seem to relax. I remember her cheeks would be pink, her eyes would sparkle as we devoured the pancakes, in two mismatched plastic chairs at the folding table in the living room."

"You two really . . . struggled, didn't you?"

"We were poor. You can say it."

"How poor?"

"No-electricity poor. No-heat-or-air-conditioning poor. Stealing-scraps-from-dumpsters-behind-restaurants poor. My mom worked two waitressing jobs just to put a roof over my head and provide enough food to survive. She drove this old extended-cab red truck that took her three years to save up for. The thing barely ran, but she loved it."

He paused and tossed another stone.

"My mom got pregnant with me at fifteen. Her parents were drug addicts, and she was well on her way to following in their footsteps. When her parents found out she was pregnant with me, they kicked her out. She had to drop out of school, lived in a halfway house for a while. Needless to say, this kind of set the tone for struggle."

"I'm so sorry. Where was your dad?"

Roman shrugged. "Who knows. I'm not even sure she knows." He scowled at me with a cross expression that dared me to judge her. "She made mistakes, but she was a strong woman, Sam."

"I don't doubt that. She must have been strong—she had you."

His jaw set, the twinkle in his eyes long gone.

"My mom was raped multiple times a day by her pimp—the guy who kidnapped me and held me for ransom—if she didn't work for him. Sometimes she was raped in the house while I was there, and other times they would take her overnight. When it happened at home, I would pull the covers over my head and cover my ears. I would never sleep on those nights. Just lay there, staring out the window until the sun came up again." The pain in his eyes was breaking my heart. "You want to know what's fucked up?"

I didn't answer as the question was rhetorical.

"Despite being raped every day, my mom would hold me, hug me, and make *me* feel safe. She always talked to me about anger, as if she somehow knew that someday, I would find out what was really happening to her. Or . . . I don't know . . . sometimes I wonder if she knew she wasn't going to survive it, and she was preparing me for it. She would tell me that no matter what happens in life, revenge is never the answer. *Rise above it, solve it*, she would say. *Solve the problem, don't be the problem.*"

Studying him, I frowned. "Do you realize you're doing exactly what your mom didn't want you to? You've dedicated your life to finding and killing Conor Cussane and getting revenge for her."

"It's different."

"Is it?"

"Conor Cussane is never going to stop. He gains more power and more followers every day, and every day, more and more women go missing. He's done to hundreds of women what his father did to my mom. He is never, ever going to stop."

"So, solving this problem is killing him?"

"Yes."

"Have you ever considered simply capturing him and then delivering him to the FBI or CIA? Is that too tame for you?"

"The man deserves to die, Sam."

"That's pretty high-handed of you to dole out life and death like that."

"It's pretty high-handed to assume another human being as your own property, Sam."

We sat in silence for a few minutes, staring at the vast jungle that lined the side of the mountain ahead of us.

This time, I picked up a rock and tossed it. "So, you drop me at the airport tomorrow, go back, kill Conor Cussane . . . and then what?"

Roman said nothing for a minute, and I got the feeling that he'd spent many hours contemplating this very question.

I pulled my legs up from the side of the rock, turned toward him, and settled in cross-legged. "Then what, Roman? Seriously? You've dedicated your life to this. Once he's dead, then what? What are you—"

"I don't know," he said.

"You need to think about it. Your entire identity, your drive, has been built around this one single goal."

Roman exhaled loudly as he dragged his fingers through

his hair. "I don't know, Sam. I don't know . . . I . . . *fuck*. Never mind, just forget it."

"Tell me." I put my hand on his arm. "Talk to me. It's okay to—"

"I don't know if I can come back," he snapped, his eyes cutting to mine like glass.

"Come back from where?"

"From all the shit I've seen and done, and what I didn't do. I don't think there's any coming back from it."

"Don't say that, Roman."

"You don't understand, Sam. Going undercover for so long changes you. The things I've seen . . ." He shook his head. "I always thought that once I killed Conor, I would be able to walk away from it all. But now I can't seem to find the line that separates me from Ardri. A part of me feels like I've turned into these men." He looked at me. "I'm one of them, Sam."

"No, you're not." My grip tightened around his arm. "If you were one of them, you would have let those men rape me. You wouldn't have risked blowing your cover to kill them."

I turned his chin to face me.

"You are innately good, Roman. In here." I tapped his heart. "You are a good man, it's just the application has gotten muddled along the way."

"What would you do?" he asked, surprising me. "What would you do right now, if you were in my shoes?"

"I would want to kill Conor, yes. But I hope I'd be strong enough to do the right thing—to rise above it."

He slowly shook his head, then with a growl, angrily pushed off the rock and strode to his backpack.

Conversation over.

That's when I realized his mind was made up. Nothing I could say would change that.

Roman would kill Conor. He would do this because he wouldn't be able to control himself. He'd get his revenge.

Exactly as his mother begged him not to do.

Roman was right. He'd gotten morally lost, twisted, in his mission to bring these evil men to justice. And I worried that it might cost him his life.

"We need to stay on schedule," he said tersely.

I stood, watching as he shrugged into his pack and pushed up his shirtsleeves, the internal torment etched across his face.

My heart broke for him. What was it like to live inside his body? Deal with that kind of guilt and unbridled anger every day?

"Let's get moving," he said.

"I need a quick second," I said, which was my code for *I need to use the restroom.*

He nodded and turned his back.

After taking one last look at the waterfall, I crossed the rock, then stepped past Roman and into the jungle. The trees lining the cliff were thin, spaced far apart, and allowed for zero privacy. I glanced over my shoulder to ensure I could still see Roman as I picked my way deeper into the brush.

Finally, I spotted a tall, thick tree with a moss-covered log fallen just behind it.

Bingo.

Untying my pants, I hastily stepped over the log, my foot twisting awkwardly on something soft.

I stumbled as I fell forward, catching myself on the log before hitting the forest floor with a hard thud, jarring my tailbone.

I gasped, gaping down at the human hand between my legs.

As if reaching for me, a long, thick, ghostly pale arm stretched along the leaves, palm up, reaching for the sky. It was attached to a body.

I scrambled backward on my butt, trying to scream but finding nothing but sand in my throat.

The man was wearing ripped army fatigues that were soiled with blood and dirt. Specks of dead leaves littered shaggy black hair that looked like tar against gray skin, almost translucent, devoid of blood.

His face was completely unrecognizable, both eyes swollen shut, each grotesquely puffy and bruised, his lips bloodied and busted. Insects swarmed his exposed skin, dipping in and out of the gaping wound that opened his throat.

The letter *C* was cut into his cheek.

"*A*re you okay?" Roman's sharp voice hardly penetrated the *whomp, whomp, whomp* between my ears.

I was lifted from the ground, then steadied by two strong hands.

"Sam—"

Startling out of my stupor, I nodded feverishly. "Yes, yes. I'm fine."

"Can you stand?" Roman frantically studied me as if I were the one on the ground with my throat slashed.

"Yes." I swatted away his hands. "I'm fine."

"Stay here."

I watched as Roman approached the corpse. His body went rigid, his face as cold as ice.

"Roman?"

He knelt down and pressed his fingers to the man's neck, despite the fact that he'd obviously been dead for some time. Roman examined the letter *C* etched into the man's cheek, then checked the man's wrists and ankles. Then he checked the man's pockets, belt, and shoes, removing something from the man's pocket and transferring it to his own. Finally, he sat back on his haunches and stared down at the dead man's face.

I knew then this was no random person.

Then, to my utter shock, Roman gently placed his hand over the man's heart, closed his eyes, and whispered a prayer.

I stepped closer, my body responding to the pain radiating off him. "Roman?"

"I need to get you out of here. Now."

He pulled his gun from its holster and surged to his feet. "Let's go."

Leaving the dead man there, Roman grabbed my hand and pulled me through the jungle. His grip hurt, the sense of urgency in his step knocking me off balance.

"Roman," I said when I stumbled. "*Roman.*"

But he ignored me, hyper-focused on the path ahead, fury swirling in his eyes.

I dug in my heels, dropped my weight, and yanked his arm. "Roman, stop!"

He whirled around.

"Who was that?" I asked.

"His name was Bear."

Bear.

"The man who was supposed to get me on an airplane and take me home?"

"Yes." He took my hand again. "We have to move, Sam."

Our pace quickened, and I had to jog to keep up with his long strides.

"Did you see his cheek?" I whispered-hissed, although not sure why.

"Yes."

"It was a *C*, right? He was branded with the letter *C*—for Conor Cussane, the CUN, wasn't it?"

"Yes." Roman's jaw twitched. "And he was tortured first. Probably for information."

My eyes rounded as I glanced around the dense forest.

"Duck," Roman said over his shoulder, yanking my arm, propelling my body downward a split second before I walked headfirst into a massive spiderweb.

I righted myself and took a quick inhale. "Do you think he told who did that to him about you—about us?"

"No."

"How do you know he was tortured?"

"His wrists and ankles were bound, and he'd been beaten."

"His throat was slashed."

"Exactly. His throat was slashed just like the men think you did to the bastards who tried to rape you, right before you escaped the lodge."

I gasped. "Holy shit."

I thought back to the conversation Roman had had with the Mexican intelligence agent and my former captor, Lucas Ruiz, where Lucas explained to us that he'd slit the men's throats to set me up and protect Roman's cover.

There was no way this was a coincidence. The guards were sending a message. Or was it Conor himself?

My heart started to race. "Do you think they know where we are? That they're watching us?"

"I don't know, Sam, but we're not waiting around to find out."

SAM

oman's pace was relentless, unyielding to the challenging terrain, my fatigue, and the elevation of the mountain we'd spent the afternoon hiking.

The stifling humidity was nothing compared to the bugs, literally swarms attacking us from all angles. Roman didn't seem to notice. He was intent on two things: keeping hold of my hand, and getting me the hell to the airport.

His demeanor had changed drastically after I found his friend's body. Roman had gone silent and cold, much like the first day we'd escaped.

Conor Cussane's father had killed Roman's mother, and now, Conor, or one of his men, had killed Roman's friend. There was no longer a question if Roman would kill the man—the question now was how long he would torture him first.

Thick clouds had moved in sometime during the hike, darkening the jungle, intensifying an already ominous atmosphere. The air was thick with tension, around us, between us. Fury radiated off Roman in waves, fear off me.

I was just about to demand a rest when Roman pivoted

suddenly, jerking my arm and leading me through thick, gnarled bushes. Ahead, dark, menacing clouds peeked between the treetops. The trees thinned and the world opened up completely as we stepped onto a large flat rock jutting out from a cliff.

A gust of wind swept past. I lifted my face to the angry clouds swirling above.

A tingle ran up my spine. Something was in the air that day, an evil so thick and heavy it felt like a third presence.

Roman stepped to the edge, scanning the landscape. Far below the cliff, the terrain evened out and appeared to be manicured in some places. We were definitely getting closer to civilization.

Closer to the airport.

Closer to the ending of us.

"There's a small township six miles east of here called Tenedores. This is where Bear was supposed to meet us."

Where Roman was supposed to "drop me," he meant.

"Once we're in town, I'll make some calls. I'll arrange a ride to the airport and another flight to get you home."

Something that resembled anger sparked in me. The Roman I got to know fishing and lying together under the stars was no more, and the hard, callous, emotionless Ardri was back. Again, he was treating me like an object.

I was no longer his sole focus. Getting to Conor was— once again. In my dream, I'd hoped Roman would board the plane with me, come home with me.

I guess not.

"I can handle it, Roman," I said. "I can get to the airport on my own once we get to town."

His head snapped in my direction. "I'll see you to the airport, where one of my men will be waiting to see you the rest of the way."

"Who?"

"Someone who's not dead."

He slipped past me, and using thick vines for support, began climbing down the side of the cliff. I followed suit, the sharp descent sending my pulse rate skyrocketing.

Finally, we reached another, much narrower ledge just below the cliff. Underneath the overhanging rock was a small cave, the entrance so small, an adult would have to enter on their hands and knees. It looked like a mouth gaping open.

The treetops blocked the view of the cave by anyone who might be searching below. It was a perfect hiding spot.

"How do you know where all the caves in this area are?"

"I studied a geological map before I came. We'll camp here tonight and set out first thing tomorrow morning." He slipped out of his pack. "You'll be at the airport before noon, home with your mother before nightfall. Stay here."

Roman ducked under the overhang, clicked on his light, and crawled into the dark cave opening. His light bounced around on the inside, and finally, he beckoned for me to follow.

I lowered onto my hands and knees and crawled through the opening, careful to avoid the sharp silt that blanketed the rock.

The cave opened up to a small space, barely enough room for Roman to stand, and no more than five feet wide. The air was delightfully cool, the rocks dry under my feet. I imagined it would be the perfect spot for a bear to hibernate.

We readied the campsite in silence, the tension thick between us. Not a single word was spoken, not a single touch. Not a single glance.

Roman left me for the first time that night. With a

loaded gun on my lap and a knife at my side, he gathered his fishing rod and hiked alone to a nearby river to catch dinner.

And for the first time since Roman had saved me, I curled into a ball and cried myself to sleep.

36

ROMAN

I tramped through the jungle, not bothering to maneuver around the dense thickets.

Anger swirled inside me as I plowed through the brush, the thorns snagging and tearing my pants. Twigs and branches popped and split as I surged through, leaving a path of destruction in my wake.

I had to get the hell out of there, away from Sam.

I was losing control. Control of everything—the mission, myself, my anger, my fucking racing thoughts.

I needed to breathe. Think. Plan and reassess. I needed to be the fuck alone, away from a woman who, with nothing but a single glance, completely derailed me.

Bear was dead. *Dead.*

My brother in arms, my friend, had been tortured and murdered for his involvement with the Samantha Greene case, the case that I'd begged him to help with. Called in a fucking favor for.

He was dead—because of me. Because of *her.*

It's her fault, I thought, stomping through the jungle.

Samantha Greene, the missing American who had

turned my life upside-fucking down. The woman had singlehandedly made me question killing Conor Cussane—the one goal I'd built my entire fucking life around.

What *the hell* was wrong with me?

Yes, it was her fault for looking at me the way she did. For touching me, smiling at me with that goddamn smile the way she did. Pushing me, poking, prodding with her damn questions. Her fault for taking care of me. Making me think I could be someone I wasn't. Making me imagine a life with her, me as her husband, a house, children, a fucking white picket fence.

Her fault for making me fall in love with her.

Then, *no*, I thought . . . *It's my mother's fault.*

Her fault for not finding a way out of her own captivity. For not going to the cops in the first place. Why hadn't she? Why had she allowed it to happen?

Because of me. Because they'd threatened *me.*

My mother had died for *me.*

Bear had died for *me.*

Fuck me, it was all *my* fault.

I was a walking fucking curse. A plague on this earth that did nothing but destroy whatever I touched.

Samantha deserved better than me. I knew this, and yet I didn't want her to leave. I didn't want her to *leave me.*

How fucked up is that?

And then what, Roman?

She would . . . what? Be my ride-or-die in a life filled with darkness and death? I couldn't put her through that. She could get hurt. The kind of life I lived didn't allow for keeping a woman.

And what if I left this life? What if I walked away? Left it all for her? Walked away from the opportunity to finally kill the man whose father had murdered my mother, and now he'd killed Bear?

Could I let my mother down? And Bear? They deserved more. They deserved justice.

A flash of white caught my eye, a vivid lightness against the impending night. I paused, squinting at the white plumeria flower peeking from the withered brush, its petals turned toward me, its leaves stretching above the bush as if searching for something.

I knelt down and studied it. It was clean. Flawless. Beautiful.

I picked it, turning it between my fingers.

It was innocent. Like Sam.

Samantha deserved more. She deserved love. Happiness. A stress-free life with someone who laughed often and made her happy. I could *never* give her that.

I surged to my feet.

What the fuck was I thinking?

What the fuck was wrong with me?

What *the fuck* was I going to do?

37

SAM

*R*oman returned long after nightfall, a bag of fish slung over his shoulder. His eyes were puffy and shaded, his skin sallow.

He paused at the cave entrance, unable to hide his surprise at the fire I'd started.

"Someone taught me how to start a fire with rocks," I said, hiding my bloodied fingertips in my pocket. Truth was, it had taken me two hours and four broken nails to start the damn fire.

Ignoring me, Roman dropped the fish at the entrance. The vile mood evident on his face permeated the small space as he grabbed his pack, retrieved the necessary tools, and then crouched by the opening. I watched him lay out each fish and begin the process of cleaning and gutting them, readying them to cook.

"Roman . . ."

His shoulders tensed. He turned his face away from me.

"Are we going to talk about this?"

"About what?" he mumbled, flaying the skin off a carcass.

"About this ridiculous tension between us."

"What tension?"

I flinched as he drew back his knife and decapitated the fish.

"*That* tension."

"There's nothing to talk about."

"Fine." I shook my head. "Fine, Roman. We won't talk about any of *that*." I gestured to the bloody carnage now covering the ledge.

Roman tossed the fish head into the trees, drew the knife back, and with a loud, violent pop, severed the head of another. I startled, my pulse rate skyrocketing, my patience obliterated.

I surged to my feet.

"I'm sorry about your friend. I'm sorry about your mom," I snapped, all my pent-up emotions exploding out of me. "I'm sorry I've screwed up everything for you. I'm sorry you took this stupid mission to save *me*, when really all you want is that goddamn USB and to kill Conor."

Ignoring my rant, Roman moved on to the next fish, his dismissal of me pissing me off even more.

"I'm sorry that all you care about is getting revenge instead of saving everyone else in that house before they get shipped to hell. I mean, are you *serious*, Roman? Your morals might not be distorted yet, but your purpose is."

Another fish was viciously decapitated, the loud pop echoing off the walls—and I fucking *lost* it.

I screamed, "You really think your mother would want you to spend your time figuring out how to kill Conor rather than saving innocent children?"

"*What*?" He threw down the knife, surged to his feet, and spun toward me, throwing open his arms. "*The fuck* did you just say to me, Sam?"

"Those children, Roman!" I shouted, refusing to back down. "You have to save them. You *have* to—"

"I *told* you, I'll deal with it after!" he yelled back.

"After you dump me at the airport? Because that's all I am? Just cargo to deliver from point A to point B?"

He blinked, his expression softening.

Absolutely seething, I stepped forward. "If you don't save those children," I angrily tapped his chest with my finger, "then I will. *I* will save them. I'll call the cops when we reach Tenedores—"

"God*dammit,* Sam. You won't."

"Yes, I will! I'll go back—"

He lunged forward like lightning. Surprised, I screamed and lurched backward but was held in place by two hands gripping my shoulders.

He yanked me to him, his eyes red with fury. "You will *not* go back to that house, Samantha." He shook my shoulders, and for the first time, I felt fear. Scared of him. "Do you understand me? You won't go back."

Tears spurted out of me in an explosion of uncontrollable sobs. It was too much. The emotions, him, everything —it was all too much.

Roman stared at me, a wild panic swirling around him. Despite the rage on his face, tears welled in his eyes.

"You won't go back," he said again, softly now, his chin trembling, the light from the fire dancing across his face.

"Why do you care?" I whispered.

"Because I don't want to lose you too!" he bellowed.

I flinched. "No. You don't care about me, Roman. It's never been about me."

He gripped my chin, tipping my head up. "It's *always* been about you, Sam. From the moment I saw you—you, *you* changed everything in an instant."

"Stop the killing," I choked out, sobbing. "Stop the death, Roman."

"Stop making me fucking crazy, Samantha." Tears rolled down his cheeks. His voice trembled. "Goddammit. I haven't felt this . . . this much . . . for anyone in my life. You don't understand—I didn't think I could feel anymore, Sam. But I do. I feel for you. You make me fucking *feel*."

I pulled his hand from my chin and pressed it against my beating heart. "You make me feel too."

"I love you, Sam, I fucking love you. And it's making me crazy."

Butterflies burst into a frenzy of flight in my stomach. "I love you too."

He fisted the back of my hair, tears running down his face. "I love you," he said again, as if he couldn't say it enough. "I love you. I love you, I—"

His lips crushed onto mine.

I stumbled backward, falling against the cave wall. My knees went weak. My world tilted as I let go. There was no more of me left to fight, to question. At that moment, I was my rawest self.

I let go.

Into his kiss, into him, I simply . . . let go.

38

ROMAN

S am's kiss was like food for a starving prisoner, heroin for a detoxing drug addict.

Her scent, her touch, the feel of her lips against mine, it wasn't enough. I wanted her, *needed* her. Needed to feel every inch of her, be immersed in everything that she was.

I threaded my fingers through her hair, cupping the back of her head, holding her in place as I felt her go weak against me.

"I'm sorry I yelled at you," I whispered against her mouth. "I love you. Please let me have you. I want you as mine. I need you, Sam."

She released a shaky exhale, her body turning boneless against me.

I wrapped my arms around her, lifted her off her feet, and lowered her to the ground. The cave walls wrapped around us like a cocoon.

The plumeria flower I'd picked slipped from my pocket, rolling onto the dark cave floor. It caught her eye. She stilled, then plucked it from the rock. Our eyes met.

"For you," I whispered.

She smiled, tears swimming again in her eyes. "Make love to me, Roman. Please. Make me yours."

Our lips never parted as we undressed each other, or as I slid the clothes under her naked body to provide padding between her and the cave floor.

Sam was intoxicating, the silkiness of her touch, the natural scent of her skin, her wild blond hair fanning out over the black rocks. It all felt so primal, awakening an animalistic need deep inside me, a feeling so different from with any other woman I'd slept with and forgotten about the next day. This feeling was one of possession, protection, pleasing the woman who was my partner. My everything.

I pinned her wrists above her head with one hand, the other, sliding over her breast. She groaned as I took a nipple in my mouth.

God, I couldn't get enough of her soft ivory skin. Of *her*.

My kisses trailed down her torso, her stomach, her abdomen, between her legs. Her body writhed underneath mine, destroying all sense of control. My heartbeat pulsed wildly in my ears, my neck, between my legs.

I tasted the inside of her thighs, opening her up to me and resting her knees against the narrowed cave walls. A feast for me.

Mine.

I lowered onto my stomach, sliding my tongue between her wet folds as I massaged her thighs.

"Roman." She breathed out my name, sliding her hands through my hair and gripping my head.

The taste of her turned me into an animal. I devoured her folds, licking the full length between her warm, wet pussy and her ass before settling on the swollen pink nub.

Her body jerked as I flicked her clit with the tip of my tongue, then softly, slowly, began to stroke it.

Pulling at my hair, she gasped for air.

I sucked the sensitive pearl, pulling her into my mouth while sliding two fingers through her folds.

"Fuck, *Roman*," she whined. She began to tremble, her heat and essence coating my face.

I wanted to drown in her.

"Come here," she pleaded. "Come here, Roman, please—"

"Not yet." I sucked, licked, reveling in these precious moments of having her absolutely submissive underneath me. "Come for me, baby. Come for—"

She screamed my name, her body shuddering under my mouth. I rode the wave with her, gripping her thighs, swallowing her release.

Finally, she stilled, her chest heaving, and contemplated me with swollen, sated eyes. I was drawn to those eyes like a magnet, crawling on top of her, my emotions whirling as passion pulsed between my legs.

No, I'd never felt this before.

Not ever.

Her hands pulled me forward. "Fuck me," she whispered, pulling me further onto her. "Fuck me now, Roman."

She arched her back as I plunged into her, her warm, wet pussy sucking me in.

My vision wavered and my breath hitched. Tingles erupted from the tips of my toes to the top of my head, my entire body responding to becoming one with Samantha Greene.

My Samantha Greene.

My mind, my thoughts, the pain, the past—the everything—it all slipped away like smoke on the wind. I was no longer in the present moment, no longer myself. Instead, I was nothing but a feeling, completely consumed by her, suspended in this perfect place, *with her.*

Tears ran down my cheeks.

We kissed, madly, passionately, as I gave her everything I had to give.

Her nails dug into my back, and her breathing hitched. "Oh, Roman . . ."

We locked eyes.

"I'm going to come again," she whispered, staring into my eyes, into my soul.

"I love you. I love you so fucking much," I whispered back, my tears dripping onto her cheek.

We shattered together, one euphoric explosion between the rocks.

I awoke in Roman's arms, engulfed in the warmth and safety that I'd become completely addicted to.

Blinking, I turned my head, surprised to see that he was still asleep. There was something about me that allowed him rest, and I loved that I could do that for him. As his chest rose and fell heavily, he was completely dead to the world.

I watched him for a while, mentally reliving the last few days. The moment I first saw him, the moment he saved me. The moment I revealed myself to him, and the moment he did to me.

And I thought about how this was the end of it.

Today was the day I would be delivered to the airport and flown back to my home. Would it be the last day I would ever see him?

A rush of sadness washed over me, followed by annoyance and confusion.

How selfish of me.

Roman had risked his life by saving mine. Children

were being held captive just miles from me. And there I was, sad and depressed that I wasn't going to see Roman again.

I turned away from him and focused on the cave ceiling.

I thought of my mom, but instead of feeling joy, I was afraid that she might have a heart attack when she saw me alive after thinking I was dead.

I thought of the children, the horrific turn their lives had taken. How many more children would be kidnapped by this group in the future? How many lives destroyed?

And why the hell was I so *sad* all of a sudden?

I should be thankful, exhilarated, excited to be pulled from hell and returned to my life. So, why *the fuck* was I so sad?

I forced myself to focus on the plan.

In hours, Roman and I would arrive at Tenedores. There, we would hitch a ride to the airport, where he would ensure I caught a flight home.

I thought of my awful appearance, my clothes. I'd have no luggage, no purse, no ID. No identification.

My identity . . . what was *that* anymore?

I reached up to touch my hair, dirty and oily.

There was Roman's pack, the bar of soap sitting inside.

I would bathe, I decided. I would clean myself up so I could face this day with courage and dignity. I would hold my damn shoulders back and walk into that airport and back into my life.

I would become an advocate against human trafficking.

I would try to forget him.

I could do this. With him, or without him—I just had to tackle *this day* first.

Inch by inch, I wriggled out of Roman's arms and slipped into my clothes. Before leaving, I placed the white plumeria flower he'd picked for me in the crook of his arm where I'd slept.

After pocketing the soap, I carefully climbed down the ravine and picked my way through the brush to the river at the base of the valley.

The woods were beginning to lighten with dawn as I stepped onto the thin, rocky shoreline. I stripped naked, taking my time to fold my clothes on a nearby branch. His clothes—ones that I would cherish forever.

I waded into the water.

Following the current, I traced the lines of the water with my fingertips until I found a deep spot. Letting myself go, I dipped under, wetting my hair.

I glanced back toward the cave, squinting through the trees. My heart literally ached at the thought that I might never see him again.

I lathered the soap, watching the foam bubble through my fingers. Slowly, I washed my hands, my arms, my shoulders, and began to cry.

I didn't want to leave him.

I didn't want to lose him.

I didn't want him to kill anymore.

I didn't want to leave, go home to a place where I knew I wouldn't be the same as when I'd left.

I stared at the blazing orange line growing on the tops of the trees, the beams of fuchsia shooting through the clouds ahead.

I wanted to stay.

I will stay, I decided at that moment.

I'd stay by Roman's side until his job was done, his mother avenged. I would stay until I ensured the children were rescued and safe.

And then we would go away together. Him and me. We

would find a place far away, a secluded, beautiful spot to build a home and rebuild our lives. Together.

Today, I would tell him I wanted to be his forever.

But I never got the chance.

The moment the sun peeked over the mountain, a hand covered my mouth. A needle slipped into my neck, and with darkness creeping into my vision, I was dragged into the shadows.

ROMAN

I could feel she was gone before I even opened my eyes.

I shot up, my instincts surging to life, instantly pushing away the haze of sleep. A flower tumbled off my chest, onto the rock. I picked up the plumeria, and my stomach dropped.

"Sam?" I yelled out, my voice echoing off the cave walls as I pushed off the rock floor.

I frantically surveyed the cave, yanking on my pants. Her clothes were gone, but her canteen, the food, my pack, everything else was still there.

"Sam?" I yelled again, noticing my pack had been moved.

I picked it up and began searching through the contents. The soap was gone.

Shit.

I spun on my heel, and leaving everything behind, scrambled down the side of the cliff and sprinted to the water. I looked at the sun through the trees, trying to get a sense of what time it was. Nine, ten o'clock in the morning? Jesus, how had I slept so long?

Sunlight sparkled like diamonds against the rushing river. A fish jumped, twisting in the air and landing with a splash. Sam's clothes lay folded on a nearby branch.

Her clothes were there—but *she* wasn't.

"Sam!" I yelled, cupping my hands to my mouth. Her name echoed off the cliff, fading into the cool morning air. A bird called out from its perch in a nearby tree.

I was alone. I could feel it in my bones.

My pulse thundered as I frantically searched for any tracks, but there was nothing.

I pulled my cell phone from the side pocket of my pants. Dead, of course, not that it mattered. I had no reception regardless.

A number of scenarios ran like a tidal wave through my head.

Someone had taken her. Or had she gone back to the lodge to save the children as she'd promised she was going to do? But her clothes . . .

Samantha had been taken, by Conor himself or one of his men.

She would be beaten for her disobedience. If not killed, she'd be put in a boat and shipped to Africa with the rest of the slaves in under twenty-four hours if I didn't get her back.

I knew then that I needed help, and there was only one place to get that.

Tenedores was roughly six miles away. The lodge, three days.

I spun around and took off running, my stomach in knots.

*N*inety minutes and six miles later, I made it to the small township of Tenedores, which consisted of a gas station/grocery store, a hole-in-the-wall mariachi bar, a liquor store with bars on the windows, a community building, and a church.

Jogging onto the pitted two-lane road, I frantically searched for any sign of Sam or Cussane's men.

An elderly couple sat on a pair of rocking chairs outside the gas station. Next door, a middle-aged woman in a vibrant multicolored dress watered flowers in front of the community building.

"Have you seen a Caucasian woman, long blond hair?" I asked in Spanish breathlessly, approaching the elderly couple.

The man and woman frowned, turning their noses up with both suspicion and repulsion. I imagined I was terrifying, soaked in sweat, covered in dirt and grime, a knife visible on my belt.

The woman who'd been watering flowers quickly tossed the hose and ran inside the community building.

"Sir," I said, directing my attention to the man, this time speaking English. "Have you seen a white woman come through here? Maybe with others? Men?"

"No." The old man narrowed his craggy eyes.

"Do you have a phone I could use?"

"No."

"No cell phone? Anything?"

"No, my wife and I have got nothin' you need, son."

I peered over the man's shoulder to a vacant parking lot where a man of about the same age was reaching for the phone, peering at me with a wary look on his face.

Shit.

The man was no doubt calling the cops, which was the last thing I needed, especially not knowing if they were on the CUN's payroll.

"Thanks, and sorry."

I waved a friendly hand to the old man and quickly pivoted, switching directions.

Keeping my head down, I crossed the street, cataloging everything around me. The blue sedan parked in front of the liquor store. The man loading grain into the back of his flatbed, the hound dog in the passenger seat. The overflowing trash can next to the lamppost.

I jogged up the steps of the small white church hidden behind the bar. When I pushed through the door, the scent immediately carried me back to my childhood when my mom had dragged me to Sunday school.

A large cross was nailed to the wall underneath the steeply pitched roof of the church. A lectern with a microphone was to the right of the cross, flowers to the left, lines of pews down the side of the room.

An old woman sat in the front row, alone.

When I strode down the center aisle, the woman turned,

her eyes sparkling as she took me in. Her face was lined with age, and her hair was perfectly fluffed and as white as snow. She was Caucasian and wore a long white dress adorned with crocheted flowers, and brown sandals on her feet.

Something dipped in my stomach the moment our eyes met.

"Ma'am . . ."

Though there was obvious urgency in my tone, I stopped at the end of the pew, careful to keep my distance and not scare her off. "Do you have a cell phone I could use?"

The woman regarded me closely for a minute, her gaze trailing over me in a way that reminded me of a mother assessing her child. Without a word, she reached into the small white clutch on her lap. Her hand trembled as she handed me an old cell phone.

"Thank you." I turned my back, clicked it on, and dialed the number I knew by heart. When the line picked up and I heard the wary *hello*, I let out a breath of relief. "Ryder—"

"Roman, what the fuck?" Ryder's voice crackled on the other end. "Where the fuck have you—"

"Ryder. Listen—I need help."

"What's going on?"

"I've been tracking a human-trafficking group called the Cussane Network, the CUN. There's this girl—Samantha Greene." I didn't need to tell him she was important to me, the crack in my voice said it all. "They've got her—took her from me. I need help, man. I need help—"

"Calm down. Where are you right now?"

"Mexico, in a small township called Tenedores. About fifteen miles from a small hangar used for private air travel. I need you here. Now. There's a lodge out in the middle of the Sierra Madre Mountains about forty-seven miles from here, near a trail called Hombre Muerto. I'll send you the exact coordinates. I need you to get there as soon as possible."

I heard the rattle of keys in the background, and a few whispers as Ryder relayed the message to the team.

"Justin's on a job," he said, "but I'll round up everyone else. What lodge are you talking about?"

"Mine."

"What? You own a lodge in Mex—never mind. Okay. Give me the lowdown of what I'm looking at here."

"The lodge is vacant aside from about four guards with guns. Over a dozen women and children, victims of human trafficking, are being held in the main basement and in various rooms. A man named Conor Cussane, the head of CUN, was supposed to arrive yesterday. I don't know if he's there, but it's best to assume he's got at least four men with him."

"So, about eight tangos?"

"Give or take. I need three things: someone at the Puerto Vallarta airport, watching for Samantha Greene. If they see her, I need them to stop her, detain her. I also need someone blocking the way to the lodge. The guards are supposed to depart for Tampico tomorrow, to a fishing dock off De Santo point. I need someone stationed there. Do not let a single woman or child step foot on any boat. And I need you to meet me at the lodge as soon as fucking possible."

I rattled off the coordinates.

Ryder's voice shook as he broke out into a jog. "I'll be on the next flight, but best guess, it will be tomorrow morning until I get there."

"Fine. Just as fucking fast as you can."

I heard doors slamming on the other end of the line.

"Does Astor know?" Ryder asked.

"About what, exactly?"

"*This*, and however the hell you've gotten yourself tied up in the Cussane Network."

"No. I've been working with them for decades."

"With them, as in undercover? Is that what you're telling me?"

"Yes."

"Fuck, Roman. Astor will have you killed if this thing blows up."

"I'll kill myself if it does. Trust me on this."

There was a moment of silence on the other end.

Then Ryder asked, "Does this have anything to do with the box that was just delivered to the office?"

"What box?"

"Yeah. This morning, a box came for you."

"From who?"

"Didn't say."

"From where?"

"Ireland."

My heart skipped a beat. "Open it."

"I'm halfway to the garage. Do you want—"

"Go back and open it now."

I began pacing as Ryder retraced his steps back into the office.

My heart pounded as I listened to the unsheathing of his knife, the rip through the packaging tape, the opening of the box.

"It's," he said, digging through the contents, "just a bunch of old shit..."

"What old shit?"

"There's a plastic bag of old pictures, an old watch, a jewelry box, a set of rusty keys..."

Memories barreled into my head like a freight train.

My mother's gold watch, her jewelry box, the keys to her old red truck.

My mother's things.

Freya.

He continued. "There's a note taped on the jewelry box."

"What does it say?"

"Hang on."

"Come on, dude . . ."

"Okay, it says," and he read . . .

Roman, this is officially my fourteenth attempt at reaching you. I have recently been diagnosed with cancer and am shoring up unfinished business, so to speak. One of many is sending you your mother's things. I truly believe she would want you to have them. She loved you so much, you know.

After my attempts to reach you failed, I decided to send them directly to the company you work for. Forgive me for sending this there, but I didn't know where else to send it. Your mother loved you, Roman. Please remember that.

— Freya

I scrubbed my hand over my mouth, contemplating the stained glass window above me, the rendition of the Virgin Mary in the middle.

"There's a letter in the jewelry box," Ryder said. "In an envelope with your name on it."

"Read it." I listened to the rustle of paper as Ryder lifted the flap. My stomach rolled as I somehow knew it was from my mother. "Wait—no. Take a picture of it and email it to me. Don't read it."

"Dude, are you fucking serious? Can't you see your secrets are getting you in trouble?"

"I don't have time for this shit right now, Ryder. Send me a goddamn picture of the letter, to my Gmail."

"Your unsecured email?"

"I don't have my fucking phone, man!" I bellowed in the Church of Christ.

There was another pause while Ryder held his tongue. "Will send it over. What are you going to do now?"

"See if my cover is still intact." Because I had no other options.

"Don't get yourself killed. See you soon, bro."

Click.

My hand trembled as I clicked into the browser, into Google, and logged into my email. Ryder's email was already there, and it had a single attachment.

I clicked it open, took a deep breath, and began to read.

*R*oman, my dear son,
I'm writing this letter, unsure if you will ever see it.

Maybe I'm writing it for myself, in a selfish confession, perhaps, as I know my time is coming. I can feel it in my bones, Roman.

I'm so sorry for what I've put you through. Sometimes, in life, we make decisions that are unclear to those around us. I want you to know that everything I did, every decision I made, was out of my love for you. And to keep you safe.

I hope you will understand that one day.

I also hope you will understand this:

I have made many mistakes in my life, but you are not one of them. You taught me that <u>our past does not define us, and that good things can come out of evil</u>.

I'll never forget the first time you asked me who your father was. I'll also never forget the guilt I felt for lying to you that day. The truth is that I do know who your father is.

When I was a young girl, I fell in love with an older man. I was much too young, much too stupid. My mother and father were drug addicts and were not present in my life. I was an angry girl. This man took me under his wing, took care of me, and I became pregnant with you at age fifteen.

After you were born, I fell in love with you. You are all that mattered to me anymore. In that one second, when you opened your eyes and looked at me, I knew I would do anything for you.

I walked away from the volatile relationship between your father and me in an attempt to raise you in a world of peace. But it was too late. Your father had become someone of power, and I know now, he never let me far from his sight. His men are the ones who took you from me that day; his men are the ones who controlled my life every day thereafter.

His men are the soldiers of the Cussane Network.

Your father, Roman, is a man named Oisin Cussane.

It was wrong of me to keep this from you. You should know who your father is.

You must also know that you have been the best part of my life. I have never regretted the decisions I made to keep you safe. You have been the steady light through the darkness. You are strong, resilient, a walking testimony to the strength of the human spirit.

Be who you are in your heart, Roman, not who the world tells you you're supposed to be.

You are not him. You are mine, my baby boy. You are you.

I love you, my son.

I am always with you, watching over you. This is my dying promise to you.

I love you.

I love you.

I love you, my dear son.

43

ROMAN

*T*he phone slipped from my hands.

I stared at the stained glass window, my vision wavering, my stomach churning, the kaleidoscope of colors merging together as one brown dizzying mass.

I killed my father.

My father killed my mother.

I'm Oisin Cussane's son.

I'm Conor Cussane's half brother, the brother of the man I've dedicated my life to murdering.

Their blood is mine, and mine is theirs.

It was as if the entire world had imploded. Everything I knew to be true—who I was, where I was from, my roots, my blood—was all lies. Devastating, crippling lies.

My ears began to buzz as I slipped into a state of complete confusion.

Who am I?

I considered my hands, my open palm, the creases running across the skin. Reality blurred. They weren't my own anymore.

Whose hands are these? Do we have the same hands, Conor and me? Does the same evil run in my blood?

I thought of all the horrible, vile things I'd done in the name of justice, of revenge. All the things I'd allowed when I should have intervened. All for the job.

I imagined my hands that I was staring hypnotically at, moving, hitting my mother, pinning her down. I thought of the adrenaline I would feel when I watched the men abuse the slaves. When I stood on the sidelines and did nothing— in the name of fucking justice.

I'm evil like them.

I am Oisin's son.

I'm a disgusting, awful creature.

I pictured my mother being thrown against the wall, thrown onto a bed.

These hands.

I pictured Sam, the fear in her eyes from inside the cage. I heard her voice, *"Get it done already . . . Just get it done."*

I saw the men attacking her, mounting her like dogs, dragging their fingernails down her back.

These hands.

My father's hands. My brother's hands.

Did he know? Did Conor know I've been hunting him for years?

Where *the fuck* was he?

Rage spun inside me, a wild, all-consuming fury.

I tilted my face to the ceiling and released a guttural scream.

44

SAM

I awoke in my cage, back in the lodge, feeling like my insides had been spread across the interstate and run over by a hundred haul trucks. I had no idea how I'd gotten back to the lodge, or how many hours or days it had been. They'd kept me drugged the entire time.

I curled into a ball at the back of my cage, hugging my knees to my chest, so incredibly nauseated.

I'd been given a yellow dress to wear—the same one the brunette had been wearing when she was shot and killed while trying to escape. My hands had been cuffed and my dog collar reattached, this time secured tight enough to feel like a fist was wrapped around my neck. It hurt to swallow, to breathe.

The children were nowhere in sight.

Men swarmed in and out of the basement, carrying boxes back and forth. The number of voices above me had doubled, along with a constant stream of pounding footsteps. The sound of engines rumbled in and out of the driveway, more loud voices, orders being yelled.

Something was happening soon.

I kept myself small, pressed into the corner of the cage. Eyes down.

The hours passed slowly. I couldn't sleep. Couldn't cry. I just sat there, staring at the bottom of my cage, dead inside.

I was sure this was it for me. And the worst part? I'd accepted it.

I didn't know where Roman was, or if he was still alive. Had they captured him too? All I knew was that this time, my hero hadn't saved me.

I'd lost all hope. In that moment, I was unquestionably ready to die.

I'd lost Roman. I'd lost my freedom again. The children were gone, probably sold or already killed.

I'd truly lost myself.

Somehow, I knew that even if I were to get out of this nightmare once again, I would never fully return mentally.

Yes, I was ready to die.

There was nothing good left of me.

45

*M*y scream echoed off the church walls as I dipped down and picked up the cell phone I'd dropped.

I turned to find the old lady was gone.

A set of car keys lay in the center of the pew where she'd sat minutes earlier, probably before I scared her to death with my scream.

I crossed the chapel, scanning the room, and picked up the keys. They were warm. Jarringly so.

"Hello?" I looked around the church, stepping onto the dais. "Ma'am?" I turned, noticing the narrow door behind the cross. "Hello?"

I knocked, then pushed open the door to what appeared to be a small office.

A middle-aged man with owlish glasses and thinning hair turned from a computer. Bars of music ran across the screen. A guitar leaned against the desk, two more on the floor next to it. He was wearing a blue T-shirt with a cartoon taco print on the front, underneath it read WANNA TACO

About Jesus? Faded jeans and flip-flops completed the man-does-not-belong-here look.

He stood, wearing a curious expression, but not fearful. Had he not just heard my mental breakdown in the sanctuary?

"There was a woman here," I said cautiously, "sitting in the first pew. I'm, uh, sorry about the scream."

"Not the first time someone has released their stress in front of the cross, my son."

It was then that I realized the man was the pastor of the church.

Shifting my weight, I held open my palm with the keys in it. "The woman—she left these and her cell phone."

"There was no woman here."

I blinked. "Yes, there—in the front row. She was wearing a white dress."

A smile crossed the pastor's face. He said nothing, just stared back at me with kind, wrinkled eyes.

I impatiently shook my hand. "She left these."

The pastor scratched the top of his head. "Well, then I guess you'd better take them, son."

"What? I—I . . ."

He chuckled.

"No," I said, growing frustrated. "You don't understand. I need to get them back to her."

"No, son, you don't understand," he said. "There was no woman here."

Frowning, I regarded the keys in my hand.

"Go on now," the pastor said. "Do what you need to get done."

I shook my head, staring at him like a dazed idiot.

"Go on."

"Thank you," I said, though it didn't feel like it fit. Nothing at that moment felt like it fit.

The pastor shrugged, then shook his head as if he weren't the one to thank.

I lingered another second before backing out of the office and into the chapel. Standing under the cross, I turned and stared at the first pew, Sam's words replaying in my head.

"You don't believe in ghosts?"

"No."

"Ridiculous."

"Is it?"

"Yes. I believe that spirits walk among us, those with unfinished business of sorts . . . Not all are evil or haunt, some are just waiting for their time to redeem themselves."

I looked up at the cross, then turned and jogged out the front door, where an old extended-cab red truck sat parked on the side of the road.

46

The basement door opened, allowing a band of light to pool into the room.

Two men entered.

I didn't recognize them, and this sent my pulse skyrocketing. I stood, readying myself for whatever was about to happen.

Their soulless black eyes locked on mine as they crossed the concrete floor.

A knot formed in my throat, hot and sticky as I stared back, pushing to a seated position in my bloodstained yellow dress. My cuffed hands threw my balance off, and I stumbled a bit before regaining my composure.

They spoke quietly in Spanish. One pointed at me as he spoke. Their gazes raked over my body, assessing.

I began to tremble, something deep in my gut telling me that my entire time in captivity came down to this moment.

The door opened again, and a dark silhouette stepped into the room. The men turned, greeting the silhouette with a subservience that I instantly recognized.

Ardri.

Roman.

My heart skipped as the silhouette stepped into the dim light. Roman was dressed to the nines in a slick black suit, a blinding-white dress shirt, and the same shiny black wingtips I remembered from what felt like so long ago. He must have had clean clothes at the lodge.

He slowly crossed the concrete, scanning each cage as he passed, not offering even a single glance in my direction.

Right now, he was not Roman. He was Ardri.

My pulse roared in my ears as the man who'd told me he loved me hours earlier neared the corner of the room. Roman spoke in Spanish to the men, his voice deep, the Irish lilt sending goose bumps racing up my arms.

One man gestured to my cage.

Our eyes finally met, mine swimming with tears, his ice-cold. He stared at me a minute.

Everyone was staring at me, I realized. My heart felt like it was about to explode.

Finally, Roman dipped his chin, ordering the men to open the cage.

"Sit," the guard demanded as he unlocked the door and swung it open.

Ducking his head, Roman stepped inside as I slowly lowered to the floor, my legs wobbling, my balance unsteady. I tucked my legs beneath me, keeping my toes flexed in case I needed to jump up at a moment's notice.

His eyes locked on mine with warning.

I had no idea what the hell was happening, just that my body was crippled with adrenaline.

My focus flicked to the two men standing outside the cage, practically panting in anticipation of what was going to happen next.

What is going to happen?

Was Roman going to beat me in front of the men? Rape me?

Instinctively, I pressed my back against the cage, pushing away from the uncertainty of the man in black coming toward me.

Roman pulled a small knife from his suit pocket, the same one he'd used to filet the fish. The same one that had sliced his thumb.

My breath caught.

"Be still," he said, his voice low and menacing.

The basement fell silent as Roman knelt in front of me, a glint of light catching on the tip of the blade.

I peeked behind him, to the men. One was grinning. Then I looked back at Roman, my eyes wide and wild with fear.

Saying nothing, Roman grabbed my cuffed arms and yanked me to him. I clumsily shuffled, regaining my balance.

He turned over my left palm, exposing the inside of my wrist, and this was when his words from our first night together echoed in my head.

"You haven't been branded?"

"Branded?"

"The CUN brands its slaves before being sold. On the inside of the left wrist, they carve the letter C."

Before being sold . . .

"No," I whispered breathlessly. Panic ran like fire over my skin. "No. Please, no, Roman."

He yanked my arm closer to him, my entire body jolting with the force.

My heart plummeted, and I began to sob. "No, Roman."

The guards snickered.

Tears rolled down my cheeks as I stared into a pair of

cold green eyes I didn't recognize. He was no longer the man I knew, the one who had made love to me under the stars. His grip tightened around my arm as the blade was pressed against my inner wrist.

"Please," I whispered, begging as a drop of blood formed under the blade.

Suddenly, he shifted his body, blocking the view of the men behind him.

The blade was lifted from my skin.

I blinked, and our eyes locked.

Positioning his arm next to mine—in a way that looked like he was holding me down—Roman used the tip of the blade to lift the cuff of his jacket.

My eyes rounded as he pierced his own skin.

"No." I tried to jerk away to stop him but was held in place by a vise-like grip.

The guards laughed, thinking I was getting sliced open.

"No, no," I whisper-hissed. "No, Roman, please don't do this . . ."

Blood popped from his skin as he slid the blade down his forearm, slicing through his own flesh.

"Oh my God." Hurting for him, I wept. "No . . ."

"Look at me," he snapped, his voice solid, despite the pain that was surely ravaging his body.

Our eyes locked once again, his jaw as tight as granite, his eyes wild, his pupils dilated as he cut his forearm. I felt his blood drip down my wrist, warm and wet.

We trembled together, sharp inhales and exhales, staring at each other, drawing strength from each other.

Blood was everywhere.

Finally, his grip loosened. He turned his cut wrist and rubbed it against my mine.

My stomach roiled. I felt the open flaps of skin smearing

against my skin as he transferred his blood onto me, making it appear that my skin had been carved as his had.

"Roman." I sobbed, staring at the blood—his blood—now covering my wrist.

"Tomorrow," he whispered back with a squeeze.

"Tomorrow?"

"Yes."

He released me, wiping the blade on his thigh. Before he pulled down his cuff to conceal his wound, I saw what he'd carved onto his wrist.

The letter *S*.

Sam.

47

SAM

I awoke to a blast of thunder rattling the windows. The gradual beat of rain on the roof turned into a loud, deafening roar. Flashes of lightning popped against the windows, followed by more thunder, like cracks of whips against brick.

Tomorrow.

Tomorrow was now today. Today, Roman would rescue me.

I sat up, searching the room for Roman, praying to see him hidden in the shadows, just waiting for the right time to unlock my cage and save me once again. Instead, I saw the twins, locked in separate cages next to each other, directly in front of me.

My heart leaped out of my chest as I scrambled across the cage. They were in bad shape but alive.

I pressed against the door, wrapping my fingers around the steel wires. "*Psst . . .*"

The girl's arm jerked at my voice, but she kept her eyes shut, pretending to be asleep, unaware I was the one trying to wake her.

Their clothes had been changed, and I realized she was in my blue housedress. The one I'd been given after being captured, the one I'd left on the bedroom floor after Roman had saved me. She was wearing my old dress while I was wearing the yellow dress the brunette had been wearing when she was shot.

Apparently, the guards simply rotated the dresses between the slaves. It made me sick.

"*Hey*," I whispered louder.

Her eyes shot open, rounding as they locked on mine. She looked at her brother, checking on him, then back to me.

"Come here. It's okay, we're alone." I gestured upward, indicating the rain. "They can't hear us."

Thunder boomed as she crawled forward, and I noticed a nasty, infected wound on her wrist.

She'd been branded. She was about to be sold.

"Is your brother okay?" I asked.

The girl shook her head, panic flickering in her eyes. "He has a rare disease. He can only eat and drink some things, and he's supposed to rest a lot. He's not doing okay."

Shit.

"I'm going to get you out of here, all right?"

She gasped, tears filling her sweet, innocent eyes. "You are?"

"Yes."

And I would. I realized in that moment that I would, *or I would die trying.*

"Soon," I said. "I promise. I'll get you both out of here."

"How?" Her fingers poked out of the cage and curled around the wire, her body trembling with hope.

"I have a friend. He's going to help us. Today, he'll get us out."

Tears streamed down her face. She began sobbing.

"Don't cry." I forced a smile, stretching my fingers through the cage. "Everything is going to be okay. I promise. What's your name?"

"Maisie."

"That's a beautiful name."

She smiled, then said, "My brother's name is Marcus. We're twins."

I laughed. "I guessed that."

"My parents . . ." She teared up. "They must be so worried. I—"

"We'll get you home, Maisie." My voice cracked with emotion. "I promise."

An echo of voices pulled our attention to the door.

"Soon." I pulled my fingers from the cage door and backed into the shadows. "Soon, Maisie."

"Thank you," she whispered before retreating to the back of her cage.

Keeping my head down, I listened to the single pair of footsteps cross the floor. One man, walking quickly.

My heart skipped a beat as a smile tugged at my lips. Roman was here to save me.

I peeked under my lashes, then frowned, blinking in surprise.

The visitor wasn't Roman, it was Lucas Ruiz.

I hadn't seen him since he'd visited us in the jungle, delivering a pack of supplies and a warning to leave. The same day I'd tried to attack him like a madwoman, not realizing he was undercover, just like Roman.

A new eye patch covered his eye. This one was dark gray like the storm clouds outside.

I glanced at Maisie before returning my gaze to Lucas. I wasn't sure which role he was in at that moment. Undercover as Capitán, or the secret agent with Mexican intelligence? The good guy or the bad guy?

Lucas's gaze locked on mine.

Roman's promise echoed inside my head. *"Tomorrow."*

Lucas hurried to my cage, glanced over his shoulder at the door, then began working the lock. "Come. Quickly."

The chain was unlatched and the door opened.

"What's going on?" I whispered, quietly stepping out of my cage.

Lucas took my hand. "I'm taking you to Roman, a few miles out."

A breath of relief escaped me.

"Wait." I jerked out of his hold and spun around.

Maisie's eyes were ablaze with hope.

"The children," I whispered to him. "Their names are Maisie and Marcus. We have to—"

"They're next. We're taking out one at a time until all the victims are saved."

I inhaled, an uncontrollable smile spreading over my face as I ran to her cage. "You're next," I said, beaming with joy.

She jumped up and looped her fingers through mine.

"You're next." Tears filled my eyes.

Maisie slapped her hands over her mouth in excited disbelief and began sobbing uncontrollably.

"Thank you," she choked out as Lucas grabbed my hand and pulled me away. "Thank you."

Smiling, I kept my gaze on hers until the door closed behind me.

48

SAM

*L*ucas and I crept through the lodge, my hand in his, my wrists still bound. I could hear the guards in the other room, laughing, talking.

I was so nervous, I thought I might have a heart attack.

Finally, we slipped out the back door.

"Run," Lucas hissed over his shoulder, his voice almost inaudible over the pounding rain.

We took off quickly, sprinting through the rain to a black four-door Nissan parked between two palm trees.

The sky was beginning to lighten in a bleak, stormy dawn. I guessed it was four or five in the morning.

When Lucas yanked open the back door, I threw myself inside. The faint smell of cigarette smoke lingered with a tropical-scented air freshener. The seat was shiny, clean, the carpets freshly vacuumed, and I got the impression it was a rental car.

"Get down," he said, slipping into the driver's seat.

I squeezed myself into the rear floorboard as Lucas settled behind the steering wheel. I didn't dare speak.

The engine hummed to life. Holding my breath, I listened to the click of the gears shifting, the grind of the wheels, the squeak of the wipers.

I didn't release my breath until we pulled out of the driveway and onto the narrow dirt road.

The wind howled against the car. Pops of lightning flickered around the upholstery like a sickening strobe light.

Finally, Lucas spoke. "You okay?"

"Yes," I whispered, though unsure why.

"Good." He tossed me a bag from the front seat. "A change of clothes are in there, plus food and water."

I pulled the bag onto the floorboard, ripping it open as quickly as I could considering my bindings.

"Deodorant, and some makeup too," he said.

I frowned, sifting through the contents. *Makeup?* My stomach tickled with an unsettled feeling that resembled nerves.

Something didn't feel right.

I pulled myself onto the back seat, grabbing the door for support as the car jostled over the pitted road.

Thunder boomed.

"Where are we going?" I asked, focusing on Lucas's reflection in the rearview mirror. His gray eye patch was wet with rain, the damp fabric streaked like a black melting candle.

"To the airport, as instructed," he said.

"Where's Roman?"

"He's meeting us there."

"Where is he now?"

"Got hung up."

My pulse rate sped up, every instinct surging to life.

A minute passed in silence.

"Have you talked to him?" I asked, suddenly desperate for Roman.

"Yes, off and on since yesterday."

"And he's okay?"

Lucas's brow furrowed in the rearview mirror, his eyes narrowing.

That increasing pulse of mine? It started to race.

Finally, Lucas spoke.

"You know," he said, his voice low and reflective. "My papa always told me that blood was thicker than water. That no matter what, family stood by each other. No matter what." His tone took on a sharp edge. "Family is all we ever have, Samantha. And disobedience to that loyalty should be punished hard and swiftly." His jaw twitched as he observed the road ahead. "It's a lesson I learned long ago."

The car bumped over a tight corner. I grabbed the door handle to steady myself, my knuckles turning white.

Lucas glanced in the rearview mirror, his one good eye meeting mine.

"Papa taught me this lesson when I was just twelve years old. You see, I'd watch him, what he did to all those women. It intrigued—fascinated—me. Every day after school, I'd sneak to the barn and watch him through the cracks. He was so strong, I remember thinking. The women, the girls, the boys, they just cowered underneath him. He *owned* them. He was so powerful."

He took a deep breath.

"Papa told me not to watch—I'll give him that. To stay away, to leave him alone. But you know, some people just don't know when to quit." His jaw tightened. "Papa removed my eye on the morning of March twenty-second. You know what happened then, Samantha? I never watched again. I learned obedience and loyalty."

My fingernails dug into my palms as I steeled myself for whatever was about to come. Because I knew then that Lucas Ruiz, the undercover agent with the Mexican government, was not who he'd said he was.

And I was in a world of trouble.

49

ROMAN

Sometime between finding out that Oisin Cussane was my father and Conor was my brother, seeing my woman caged again, and slicing open my arm for her, the mission became muddled. All plans vanished, along with the feeling of need for them.

My entire life revolved around one thing. Saving Samantha. That's it.

I was living minute to minute, a loose cannon operating on emotions, not facts and figures. There was no cool, calm head anymore, just a savage need to protect what was mine.

It went against everything I'd been trained.

It was, without question, the most dangerous place I'd ever been. This is when mistakes happen, missions derail, lives are lost.

And the worst part? I didn't even realize it.

I slipped behind a tree as two taillights disappeared down the dirt road. A black four-door Nissan, best I could tell.

The guards were headed to the port. Soon, a trailer full of slaves would follow.

I needed to hurry.

Once the car was out of sight, I refocused on the lodge and picked up my pace, slipping from tree to tree, careful to stay in the shadows.

I'd parked the pickup truck in a thicket of ferns a half mile back to avoid being seen. It would be a difficult trek for Sam once I rescued her, but it was the safest option.

She could do it. She was strong.

Rain poured off my nose, my fingertips. My black suit was saturated, the wound on my wrist stinging with each rub of the fabric.

She was worth it, though. Every fucking second of that pain. And now I would never forget her. She was etched forever into my skin.

Sam.

Feeling my heart beat faster, I pushed into a jog, something in my gut triggering a sense of panic that I didn't like.

Minutes later, I approached the lodge.

The front door opened and two guards in army fatigues stepped outside, huddling under the small overhang to light a cigarette. I took a quick inventory of the vehicles. Most I recognized, but one SUV was unfamiliar.

Had Conor Cussane finally arrived? Had *my brother* arrived?

The thought nearly sent me lunging out of the shadows, guns blazing, mowing down everything in my path until I reached him.

Sam.

Sam first.

Sam, Sam, Sam.

Adrenaline surged through my veins as I skirted the edge of the lodge, careful to avoid the line of sight of the guards smoking their cigarettes.

Thunder rumbled in the distance, less angry now. The storm was moving away. Taking my chances, I ducked down and darted across the small yard that led to a side door that I knew was close to the basement.

Although I didn't have a plan if I got caught, I didn't care. I'd defend myself, lethally if necessary, or improvise as needed. Getting Sam into my arms was my only goal.

I pushed open the side door and stepped inside, ready for what might come. The hallway was empty. A light shone from the kitchen, where overlapping chatter echoed and shadows moved along the walls.

I could *feel* the anxiety in the house. Yes, they were loading up and heading out. And they were scared.

My heart pounded as I slipped down the hallway and through the basement doors. The space was rank with fear. As I jogged across the basement, slaves whispered and moaned, a few sobbing in my wake. They knew something was coming.

I ignored them, focused on the last cage in the corner. But the cage was empty.

My stomach dropped.

I spun around, meeting two huge blue eyes staring back at me.

"Where did she go?" I asked, panic tightening my voice.

"The man came and took her," the girl whispered back.

Panic shot through me—had Conor taken her?

"What man?" I asked.

"The man they call Captain."

Captain?

Lucas?

I blinked.

But he's supposed to have already left, supposed to be sitting at the bedside of his pregnant daughter.

"Capitán took her?" I asked, trying to understand.

"Yes. The man with the eye patch."

Definitely Lucas.

I frowned, saw Sam's empty cage, then looked back at the girl. "When? How long ago?"

"Just ten minutes, maybe fifteen."

I thought of the black car driving away from the lodge. Why the hell had Lucas taken Sam? And where the fuck was he going with her?

Something was wrong. Very, very wrong.

I spun on my heel.

"Sir . . . sir!" The little girl whisper-shouted at me, stretching her fingers through the cage. "She promised someone would save us today."

I stopped and turned. There was no way I had time to save the children, to carry them a mile to my truck and then begin to find Sam.

"*Please*, sir," the girl pleaded.

A loud bang sounded above, followed by sharp voices.

I tore myself away from the teary blue eyes and jogged up the stairs, forcing myself to ignore the pleas behind me.

There was no time. All I cared about was Sam.

I slipped down the hall, retracing my path. The cell phone in my pocket buzzed, startling me. I lunged into a vacant room and pulled it from my pocket.

UNKNOWN CALLER flashed on the screen of the old lady's phone, with only a single bar of reception.

I answered.

"Roman . . . landed . . . the airport." Ryder's voice crackled on the other end. He'd redialed the number I'd called him on from the church. "I . . . letter . . ."

"Hang on," I said, "I can barely hear you."

I jogged across the room and pulled open the window. One of the many peaks that topped the lodge was just to my left, its tip leading higher up the roof.

"Hang on," I said before stuffing the phone in my pocket.

Gripping onto the window frame, I climbed out. Rain dripped from the leaves overhead as I carefully crept along the siding. Pulling myself up and onto the peak, I crawled up the side of the roof, to the top.

Ryder was yelling my name by the time I finally returned to the call.

"You there? *Roman*—"

"Yeah, bad reception. Where are you?"

"Listen, about the letter in that box—"

The letter from my mother, confessing that my father was the leader of a human-trafficking network.

"You read the letter?" I snapped.

"Of course I read the fucking letter, dude. You've obviously got yourself in a shit-ton of trouble. I don't give a fuck who your father is. We're a team, man, fucking ride or die."

I inhaled, the relief overwhelming.

"Listen," he said. "I'm heading to the lodge as fast as I can, but I've got news for you. I had one of my old DOD contacts reach out to your contact in G2, the Irish military intelligence division."

I repositioned, straining to hear Ryder over the rain and shoddy reception.

"I requested the file on your father, Oisin Cussane, to study on the plane ride down. You probably know it's rumored that he has had, like, a dozen illegitimate children with his mistresses, right?"

"Yeah, like me."

"Well, my goal was to begin pinning down all these

people, assuming that they could be involved in this mess in one way or another. I found something interesting. According to the file, Oisin is rumored to have actually claimed one son, to train him to take over his organization if anything ever happened to him. Thing is, the kid's name was kept under wraps, and there's no documentation connecting him to the birth, or anything."

"Except . . ." Obviously, Ryder had something.

"Except an old medical record that was attached to Oisin's file with an asterisk. Meaning, they couldn't confirm the validity of it, but felt it was important enough to keep record of."

"What is it?"

"Thirty-five years ago, a boy, age twelve, was admitted into an emergency clinic somewhere outside of Dublin. The file says he was alone, delirious, close to death. The boy claimed he was the son of Oisin Cussane. Kept screaming it over and over."

"What was wrong with him?"

"His left eye had been carved from his head."

I spun around, almost losing my footing as I stared in the direction of the black car I'd seen disappearing into the rain.

"The man came and took her."

"What man?"

"The man with the eye patch."

Lucas, my friend, my confidant.

Lucas Ruiz, a fucking liar, a fraud. My partner for over a decade wasn't undercover with the Mexican government. He was Conor Cussane, Oisin Cussane's son, undercover within his own organization. The man that no one had laid eyes on, the man who ruled a multimillion-dollar organization from behind the secrecy of his laptop.

Conor Cussane, the mystery, the enigma.

My brother.

And he had Sam.

I killed the call, clambered down the roof, and sprinted to my truck.

50

*M*y mind raced to put together this complex puzzle, but one thing was certain—Roman and I had been fooled, and there was no telling what trap he'd walked into now.

The thought that something had happened to him absolutely sickened me.

"Who are you, Lucas?" I asked. "Because I know you're not with the Mexican intelligence agency."

"You're wrong. I'm with the CNI. I'm also Oisin Cussane's son," he said proudly, as if I should be proud as well.

My eyes closed, dread washing over me like a wet blanket.

"You're . . . Conor Cussane," I said, my voice trembling.

"That's correct. However, according to the Mexican government and the CUN, I'm Lucas Ruiz."

Confused, I shook my head, trying to solve this riddle. "But the guards in the lodge didn't refer to you as Conor, they called you Capitán."

"Because they, along with the government, don't know who I really am, *mi amor*."

My love. My stomach roiled.

"We have a legacy to uphold, my papa and I, and many men want me dead. After Roman killed my father, I went undercover within my own organization, creating an alter ego of myself to weed out the rats and weaklings, while keeping myself—his legacy—safe. I moved our operations to Mexico, where I joined the CNI to keep an eye on the Feds. It was the only way I could keep his legacy alive. This is how I grew the organization to what it is today."

"You played Roman," I said, seething.

"No, no, no," Conor said with an evil laugh. "He played me, *mi amor.* I truly believed blood was thicker than water until I realized my brother had dedicated his entire fucking life to killing me. His own blood. He killed *my* father." His nostrils flared with emotion. "His own fucking father. It is the ultimate betrayal."

My jaw dropped and my breath caught. "You're Roman's brother?"

"Half brother. His mother was a whore from Ireland, my mother a businesswoman from Mexico—or was, I should say. She died five years ago."

"How long have you known Roman was your brother?" I asked breathlessly.

"A few days after we first met, both undercover, at a sale in Guatemala."

"A sale of women?"

"Yes. After I noticed his Irish accent, I began digging. What were the odds that this Irishman who was so inter-ested in my father and the CUN, was both born and bred in Ireland? I knew something was up. I found Roman's birth certificate, and his mother's name. Then my father's right-hand man confirmed that Roman's mother had been one of my father's many mistresses. That's when I learned the truth. After that . . ." Conor angled his head to the side. "It became a fun game, me watching him hunt me. Can you imagine?"

A cold sweat broke out over my body.

"I planted false intel, leaked videos of slaves, watched him chase his tail for years . . . until he started getting too close. A relentless son of a bitch, he is, and a pain in my ass. He had to be disposed of."

Disposed of.

"No—please. Don't," I begged. "He doesn't know you're his brother. Please, just—"

"He will once I offer your life for his."

My heart stopped. "*What?*"

"The moment I heard the US government had hired my brother to find you, Miss Samantha Greene, one of my slaves, the game began." He laughed, an evil maniacal laugh. "But then, when I saw the way he looked at you, when I saw how possessive he was when he spoke about you, I knew the game had taken a turn. He is in love with you, *mi amor*. I knew the moment I saw him look at you."

Conor glanced in the rearview mirror.

"He will find us, *mi amor*. When he does, I will offer to release you in exchange for his life. He will kill himself to save you because that's the kind of idiot he is. He is weak. He is not a Cussane."

"You're a sick fuck."

"That I am. I truly, truly am, *mi amor*. I know this."

"Where are you taking me?" I asked, slipping my bound hands onto the door handle. Locked, of course. I searched out the window for Roman, for help, an idea, anything.

An eerie blue glow was pushing through the darkness of night. The storm had relented, leaving a growing fog in its wake.

"We'll go to Africa to start, then Thailand. I have new operations starting there. You'll be mine. We'll live by the ocean and have a good life. Together, we will have many children to carry on the legacy."

"I will *never* bear your children," I spat out.

Conor looked in the rearview mirror, his wicked, slitted eye fixing on me. "It is not your decision."

Yes. It. Is.

I reared back, slamming my feet into the back of his seat.

"What *the fuck*?" he bellowed, bouncing against the seat.

Again and again, I kicked the seat like a mule, releasing the rage boiling inside me. The car swerved back and forth, sliding on the mud.

Conor flung his fist back to hit me, but accidentally slammed the gas in the process of half turning.

The car lurched forward, its tires spinning. The wheel yanked, sending us off the road and slamming into a tree.

My body was propelled forward, flying into the front seat. Scrambling, I yanked the door handle and threw myself out. Unable to use my cuffed hands to cushion my fall, I landed face-first with a thud on the muddy road, my yellow dress snagging against the door frame.

Conor caught my ankle.

I twisted painfully, squinting at the man who I knew, with certainty, would be the end of me. His face was bloodied, contorted with rage.

"Come back here, you fucking bitch."

I writhed and bucked as Conor slithered his way over the console and across the passenger seat, a tight grip around my ankle.

When he crawled on top of me, Roman's words echoed through my head.

Fight, Samantha. Fight.

And I did. I fought like a wild animal.

I fought until Conor wrapped his hands around my throat, cutting off my air supply.

51

ROMAN

I raced the borrowed red truck out of its hiding spot behind the trees and fishtailed onto the narrow dirt road, heading in the direction that I'd last seen the black car that held Lucas Ruiz—aka Conor Cussane, my brother—and Sam.

What remained of the thunderstorm dripped in heavy, bloated drops from the thick canopy overhead, blurring my windshield. A thick fog had settled between the trees, snaking in and out of the ferns and making visibility shit.

I pressed the accelerator, driving far too fast for the conditions, fixed on finding that fucking car.

The truck skidded around a sharp corner, sending mud and rock spinning from my tires, ricocheting off the trees like gunshots. Ahead, two taillights glowed through the murky gray mist.

I punched the gas, not realizing the vehicle ahead was stopped until I was almost on its bumper. I hit the brakes just as a gut-wrenching scream echoed through the fog.

Sam.

I jumped out of the car, sending the driver's door popping on its hinges. The fog was as thick as smoke. The *ding, ding, ding* of the open-door alert carried on the air like a warning.

The scene unfolded around me bit by bit, the fog slowly revealing the scene of the wreck. The black sedan had hit a tree and was halfway in a ditch, both the driver's and passenger side doors standing open.

The car was vacant.

"Sam!" I screamed.

"*Roman!*"

I froze, then spun around, pivoting away from the car and following her voice.

"Sam!" I jogged, my eyes wild and wide, trying to see through the goddamn fog.

An arm shot out of the mist, and then as if in slow motion, the silhouette of a man appeared, his head, shoulders, torso.

Lucas. Conor. My brother.

In that moment, I saw myself in him, and suddenly everything clicked. The guards at the lodge thought I was Conor because of my physical resemblance to the rumored description of the man. I'd never noticed it before. The nose, the eyebrows, the build. And I had the suit, the money, the self-assurance carried by someone of power.

What a mindfuck.

Conor was on top of Sam, who was writhing in his hold, her yellow dress saturated in mud and grime.

Rage exploded inside me.

This man's father had killed my mother and obliterated what I knew to be family. This man had destroyed countless other families too, lives, daughters, wives.

He'd fucking tricked me. Played me.
More than all that, though—
This man had my fucking woman.

52

SAM

I could no longer feel Conor's grip around my throat or the burn in my chest as my lungs screamed for oxygen. I could no longer hear my heartbeat, or his heavy breathing.

The world around me faded, and black dots slowly creeped into my vision.

But then, like a dream, I saw Roman through the fog, his massive silhouette pushing aside the gray mist like tendrils of smoke.

He came for me.

My mouth opened as I tried to scream out to him. My fingertips reached but felt nothing. My legs wanted to move but couldn't.

Bright pops of light began bursting in my vision. I heard the deep baritone of his scream, but my brain couldn't register the words.

Then darkness took over.

Suddenly, my body was jolted, nails ripping open the skin around my throat as Conor was pulled off my body.

Gasping for breath, I pulled my knees to my chest,

rolling onto my side in the fetal position, sucking air that my lungs weren't making room for.

Both men landed with a thud on the ground a few feet next to me, immediately engaging in hand-to-hand combat. Roman and his brother, fighting to the death.

I forced myself to a seated position, painfully swallowing the bile that rose with the rush of nausea. My throat was on fire.

Both men were on their feet now, viciously beating each other to a bloody pulp.

I felt drunk, my brain not quite catching up with the adrenaline beginning to stir inside me. But I knew I needed to get to Roman. To help him.

Standing was out of the question, so I crawled across the mud on my hands and knees, my vision blurred, my pulse a deafening *whomp, whomp, whomp* in my ears.

Roman's body slammed against a tree. Blood dripped from his chin.

Conor didn't relent, advancing on Roman like a wild animal. He kept screaming, "You were my blood, you were my blood."

Roman swung a punch and missed. His steps faltered against Conor's rapid-fire punches, the rage pouring off the evil man like an invisible force.

I tried to stumble to my feet but collapsed again onto my hands and knees.

I heard a loud pop of fist against bone, and then, like a tree falling, Roman went down like a plank, his body disappearing into the thick brush.

"No!" I screamed in a pathetic gargled hiss.

Conor turned to me. His eye patch had fallen off during the fight, revealing a scarred black hole where his left eye should have been. Blood poured out of his mouth, and one of his bloodied teeth was missing.

His chest heaving, he stumbled over to me, his eye sparking with that same feral rage as when he'd looked at Roman.

I scrambled backward, willing my body to leap up and run away from this horrifying monster advancing on me.

"Oh no you fucking don't." Conor lunged forward, his bloodied face contorted with rage.

I screamed, bracing for the attack, but my attention was pulled behind the madman.

Roman leaped from the brush like a lion, slamming his fist into the side of Conor's head, the vicious blow sending Conor flying into the air like a rag doll.

Roman fell to his knees next to me. "Are you okay?" He frantically looked me over.

My chest heaved as I stared into his bloodied face and frantic eyes, unable to form words.

"*Sam*, are you—God, tell me you're okay." Roman desperately gathered me into his arms.

I nodded and opened my mouth to speak, but something pulled Roman's attention away from me.

Conor had emerged from the fog and was scrambling to his car on all fours.

Roman's fingers slipped from my body, his grip around me released. I collapsed back onto the ground. Wild-eyed, Roman turned his back to me.

He didn't hear my grunt of pain as I hit the dirt. He no longer saw me.

I was no longer his focus. I no longer existed to the man.

His eyes were unlike anything I'd seen before. His face was absolutely terrifying.

Conor reached his car, throwing himself inside and slamming the gas.

Roman turned toward a truck, which was running, ready, the door standing open as if calling to him.

My stomach sank. *He's going to leave me.* Roman was going to catch Conor and kill him, avenge his mother, avenge Bear, and finish the job he'd built his life around.

I no longer existed in his world.

And it broke my fucking heart.

53

ROMAN

a tornado of hate, adrenaline, pain, sadness, and guilt spun through me as I watched my brother pull himself into his car. He was wounded badly and probably experiencing the onset of a concussion.

I watched the door slam, his silhouette slumped over the seat.

This was it. My moment.

My chance to kill one of the most ruthless human traffickers in the world. Kill the son of the man who'd killed my mother, and who had killed my friend. This was my moment to kill my brother and reset the family legacy.

Images of my mother flashed in front of me like an apparition in the fog, her voice a slowly haunting song in my head.

"Revenge is never the answer. Rise above it. Solve it."
"Solve it."

I looked back at the woman on the ground, more words suddenly echoing in my ear, but this time it wasn't my mother's voice, it was Sam's.

"There's got to be a point where you just have to let it go, Roman. Let it all go."

"Let him go."

I didn't hear the tires spin as Conor hit the gas, didn't feel the rocks pelt my face.

I stared down at Samantha Greene, and for the first time, felt the mission fade away.

Felt everything fade away.

With her.

54

SAM

I knew the minute his decision was made. I knew by the warmth in his eyes and by the butterflies that burst to life in my stomach.

Roman wasn't leaving me.

"I love you," I whispered breathlessly, tears spilling down my cheeks.

Tears filled his eyes as he dropped to his knees once again and pulled me back into his arms. "I'm sorry, baby, I'm so sorry." His gaze narrowed on the damage to my throat from Conor's nails.

"Stop." I cupped Roman's cheeks and forced his eyes back onto mine, studying his swollen, bloodied face.

He'd chosen me. Roman had renounced his mission, his vengeance, his life-long goal, for me.

"Your mother would be proud," I said.

"No." Carefully, he lifted me to a seated position, wrapped me in his arms, and stood, cradling me like a baby.

"No?" I frowned.

"No. Not yet. Let's go get the children."

"Oh, Roman." I threw my arms around him, a rush of

energy and excitement blowing through my body. "Have they been taken away yet?"

"No. I've got people stationed at both the airport and the dock. They would have called me."

"Then what are we waiting for?"

"Just this second." He exhaled, then kissed my nose. "Just this second."

My smile faded as I considered his bruised, dirty face. "Are you okay?"

"Yeah."

"Hell of a fight."

"Yeah. He's definitely my brother."

I laughed. "Well, you got him in the end."

Roman didn't respond. Instead, he carried me across the dirt road.

But Roman didn't get him in the end because he let him go—for me. I wondered if he would ever regret that decision.

"Where did you get the truck?"

"Divine intervention."

I cocked a brow. "God gave you the truck?"

"Something like that."

"Well, can he turn it into an army of soldiers to defeat the guards, then into a jet to zoom us all away?"

"At this point," Roman peered down at me, "I don't know what the hell to expect—from me, or anyone else for that matter."

He slid me into the passenger seat, taking time to buckle my seat belt and make sure I was comfortable. After making a U-turn, we took off, speeding down the dirt road to the lodge.

The clouds overhead were dissipating. The early morning sun was beginning to peek through the cracks, like golden swords of fire spearing down from the sky. I imagined the beam of light a supernatural army, readied to support us for this final mission.

Four vehicles were parked in front of the lodge, and next to them, the same U-Haul that had transported me days earlier. They were preparing to load up the slaves.

We were out of time.

"Get down," Roman said.

We drove past, turning into a narrow clearing a few yards from the lodge, and parked behind a group of trees.

"What's the plan?" I asked, my body thrumming with adrenaline.

"You're staying here."

"Absolutely not."

"Sam—"

"Roman, I am *not* staying here. You need me, and you know you do. You can't kill all the guards yourself, and then get every one of those slaves out of there alive. Who knows how many guards are inside, or on their way here."

Roman glanced in the rearview mirror, then scrutinized the lodge, a deep line of concentration forming on his brow. I was right, and he knew it. There was no way he could do this and make it out of there alive.

He looked at me. "What do you suggest, Rambo?"

"Well, I'm glad you asked, because I actually do have an idea. I want to create a diversion."

"A diversion?" His eyes narrowed.

"Yes. Me."

"Abso-fucking-lutely not."

"You got a better idea? Listen, I'll create a diversion—we know there's nothing more these guys want than me, the one who killed their comrades and got away—*twice*. I'll let them spot me in the woods, and when they come after me, you go get the children in the basement."

"And then what, Sam? What the hell do you think you're going to do then? When they're chasing after you in the jungle?"

Frowning, I chewed on my lower lip. "I haven't gotten that far yet."

"Well, you won't get that far because you'll be dead."

I threw up my hands. "What the hell else are we going to do? And we're losing time just sitting here."

Roman stared again at the lodge, his mind racing. All of a sudden, he blinked, his hand patting the side pocket of his tactical pants.

His brows arched, a wicked sparkle in his eye.

"You've got an idea."

"I do." He reached into his pocket and pulled out a shiny silver ball, cupping it in the palm of his hand.

"What is that?"

"You were a softball all-star, right? In college? Pitcher?"

"That's right." I was skeptical where he was going with this. "A long time ago. I even named my dog after Dot Richardson."

His brows arched. "Ah. I wondered where the hell Richard came from."

"I can't believe how much you researched about me."

"I couldn't stop."

I smiled at that.

"Anyway," he said, "you think you've still got it in you? That all-star pitcher's arm?"

I thought back to a time when I was truly happy, with my friends, early summer mornings on the field. Back when I loved what I did, when I kicked ass at it. I thought of the Converses sitting in my closet, the dust collecting on them.

That tingle I would get as I stepped onto the mound vibrating through my body.

A wicked grin curved my lips. "Hell yeah, I do."

He grinned back. "Thought so." He examined the ball. "This is called a bulldozer. It was Bear's."

My eyes rounded. Not only did the weapon belong to his deceased friend, but it sounded extremely lethal.

"Have you ever heard of confusion silencers?" he asked.

"No, but it doesn't sound like a big warm hug."

"No, it's actually quite the opposite." He looked down again at the ball. A smile cracked his lips. "Bear loved these damn things. Snuck extra out of the utility closet every time we were deployed. He used them all the time."

"What are they?"

"When this little button is pressed," Roman indicated a button on the side, "you have three seconds to throw it. Once it hits the ground, the impact sets off a deadly explosion—but not just of fire and smoke. It releases a jarring, paralyzing sound that is literally so high that it can make you throw up. The blast will probably kill them. If not, it will completely immobilize your attackers for at least two minutes, allowing you to get away."

"Holy shit."

"Tell me about it. The key is you have to get away before the bomb detonates. Three seconds to travel as fast as your feet can carry you, then hide and cover your ears."

My heart started to pound, and I swallowed deeply. "I can do this."

"I know you can," he said, his eyes leaving no question that Roman truly believed I was strong enough to do it.

And that is the moment that I had no question he was the man for me.

I wasn't weak. I didn't need to be coddled. I was strong. I

wasn't a fucking damsel in distress. I was a fucking badass. I was his partner.

We. Were. Partners.

I opened the palm of my hand, and he rolled the ball from his hand into mine.

"Here's the plan," he said quickly, urgency back in his voice. "You're going to do exactly as you said—you're going to make yourself seen in the woods. Make noise, whatever. When they come after you, take off running in *this* direction, toward the truck. The moment the guards take off after you, I'll sneak in the back and get the children."

He hesitated, his jaw hardening to granite.

"Stop, Roman." I placed my hand over his. "Please. Don't doubt me. I can do this—we can do this."

He softly cupped my cheek, nodded, then continued.

"Once they start chasing you, I want you to run like hell and count to five. Then I want you to press the button and throw this ball as hard as you can at the men. You have three seconds to get as far away as possible and take cover and cover your ears. The sound only lasts a few seconds. Then get up and run like hell back to the truck. I'll meet you here with the children."

I nodded, my heart beating like a jackhammer.

"What if someone stays in the house," I asked. "What if they all don't come after me? And you get attacked?"

"I'll take care of them *and* whoever—if anyone—survived your attack."

"What about the other slaves?"

"We'll intercept them later on the road when I meet my team. We don't have time to go back and forth. The children are this mission's priority."

"Okay." I nodded, then inhaled. "Let's do this."

I put my hand on the door handle, then paused and

glanced over my shoulder—into an intense, piercing green gaze.

"Let's do this," he said, that gaze making my stomach flip.

"Let's do this for the kids, for your mom, and for Bear."

"I love you, Sam."

"I love you, Roman."

We kissed desperately, passionately, like two lovers just before approaching the battlefield.

We met at the hood of the truck. Nerves vibrated inside my body.

"We're going to split up here. I'm going to skirt around to the opposite side of the lodge," he said, then regarded me with more intensity than in the truck. "Tell me the plan again."

I nodded. "I'm going to make myself seen, run for five seconds, then push the button and throw the grenade. I have three seconds to get away, get down, and cover my ears. Then I run like hell back here, to the truck."

"Exactly."

He cupped my cheek and kissed me one more time. "I'll see you soon, my love."

Grenade in hand, I took off jogging, low and fast, as Roman disappeared into the shadows.

Darting through the spears of light, I ran like an animal. Adrenaline, hope, and a certainty that I was doing exactly what I needed to do at that moment carried me like wings on my feet.

Something came over me as I ran through the jungle. My nerves evaporated, an inner grit thrumming through my veins. I felt emboldened, and in a crazy way, I felt like I was becoming the person I was meant to be.

I felt like I was getting my own form of revenge.

The fog was burning off but still lingered, creating an obstacle for allowing the guards to see me. I kept glancing over my shoulder for Roman. Of course, he was long gone.

I focused on the weapon in my hand, the strength of it. The strength of the woman carrying it.

Finally, I reached the lodge. My chest heaving and adrenaline roaring, I peeked from behind a tree, getting the lay of the land. Two men stood guard on the deck outside, and another silhouette moved inside.

Nerves fluttered inside my stomach.

My gaze dropped to the ground below the lodge. Below the heavy, wet soil lay the basement where I'd been held, countless women had been held, and two innocent children were still being held as slaves.

Setting my jaw, I narrowed my eyes on the guards. Hate boiled in my veins.

Here I am, motherfuckers.

I stepped out from the cover and began moving along the tree line. Not two seconds passed before one of the guards spotted me, shouting to his comrades. More shouts, then all hell broke loose.

I spun on my heel and took off like a rocket. Angry voices yelled out to me, footsteps pounded the ground.

I began counting.

Five . . .

Four . . .

Three . . .

Two . . .

I planted my feet.

One . . .

Lifting the grenade, I pushed the button.

I turned and hurled the ball at the three men sprinting

toward me. Spinning on my heel, I lunged forward, slipping on the wet earth before taking off again.

Three . . .

Two . . .

I leaped over a fallen log, dropped to the ground, and covered my ears.

One.

The explosion shook the ground, followed by cracks of tree limbs breaking.

Even over the blast, I could hear the sounds of the screaming men, the retching as they vomited, the weight of their bodies hitting the ground.

Joy, hysterical jubilation, ignited inside me. I pushed off the ground and looked over my shoulder at the ball of smoke before racing back to the truck.

I did it. I did it.

We did it.

Back at the truck, I checked over my shoulder, searching for any signs that I'd been followed. Once I was sure I was alone, I slid inside the cab, locked the door, hunkered down, and kept my eye on the tree line, waiting for Roman and the children to emerge.

I waited.

And waited.

And *waited.*

Nerves bubbled up, quickly turning into panic.

Something had happened. Something bad. I needed to get back there.

I searched the truck for any kind of weapon but came up short.

Fuck it, I thought, gripping the door handle. *I'll fight with my fists.*

As I was pulling the door handle, Roman emerged from

the trees, cradling the boy in his arms. Maisie was at his side.

I jumped out of the truck, tears filling my eyes.

Maisie ran into my arms and began sobbing. "Thank you, thank you, thank you."

Squeezing her tightly, I looked at Roman, at the boy in his arms. Marcus was pale, his lips a bluish gray. He needed immediate medical attention.

My eyes met Roman's. He dipped his chin, confirming this thought. We needed to get him to a hospital—now.

"Get in, get in, quickly," I whispered, ushering Maisie inside the cab while Roman carefully laid Marcus in the back seat.

Once the children were secure, Roman slid into the driver's seat, fired up the engine, and hit the gas.

"Are we out?" Maisie asked from the back seat, her voice trembling. "Are we safe?"

Roman and I glanced at each other but said nothing, knowing we weren't out of the woods yet.

55

SAM

*W*e were silent in the truck, waiting on pins and needles to breach this godforsaken jungle and have a clear shot to the airport.

"What is that?" Maisie asked, peering from the back seat.

Frowning, I leaned forward, studying the black smoke rolling up from the trees in the distance. "That's not fog."

"No. It's a fire," Roman said, his voice suddenly low and uneasy.

"Fire? Like a forest fire?"

He shook his head. "No. Not trees, something with chemicals—you can tell by the color of the smoke."

My pulse picked up, an instinct stirring. "Is there a way around it?"

"No. There's only one road to and from the lodge. This fire is on purpose."

Shit.

"What are you going to do?"

"Get through it." Roman glanced over his shoulder. "Maisie, get yourself and your brother down into the floorboard. Cover your heads and get as small as possible."

"I'll get back with them," I said, unbuckling my belt.

I climbed over the seat, dropped to my knees, and folded myself over the children, providing a shield for whatever might come our way.

I kept my head up, peeking between the seats at the windshield. The cloud of smoke grew bigger and darker, puffs of ink against the vibrant greens of the jungle canopy.

"It's right around this corner," Roman warned, braking.

I lifted up, peeking over the seat.

"What the . . ." I frowned, blinking wildly, thinking that surely I was seeing things.

Three massive men blocked the road like sentinels, their arms crossed over their chests, a burning ball of carnage at their back.

It wasn't until a gust of wind blew the smoke that I realized the burning object was a car. A black four-door sedan.

Conor.

"Who are they?" I whisper-hissed from the back seat.

Roman slowed, maneuvering into the ditch. "Friends."

Friends?

I gaped at the three men, each more massive than the next. All three had the same menacing, intimidating, terrifying vibe that Roman carried.

Each was as handsome too.

"Stay here." Roman turned off the truck and climbed out of the driver's seat.

"Stay here," I said to the children, following suit.

Roman glanced over his shoulder, smirking at my defiance, and I winked. He waited for me to catch up, then returned his focus to the fearsome men ahead of us.

"Talk about comin' in hot," he said.

"You look like shit." The tallest man stepped forward, shaking Roman's hand.

"Mack," Roman said, then glanced at the other man. "Ryder. Thanks for showing up."

The man he referred to as Mack was built like an ox with wide, massive shoulders that stretched the fabric of his army-green T-shirt. His short, unkempt brown hair matched the stubble on a square chin and thick neck.

Ryder, a few inches shorter than Mack, carried the same rugged handsomeness as his counterpart, but with a bit less unbridled, angry testosterone rolling off him. I noticed a wedding band on his finger.

Who's this?" Roman nodded to the youngest of the group, but no less terrifying.

"New guy. Phineas Decker. A Farm recruit."

"CIA?"

Phineas nodded, scanning me in a way that suggested the guy missed nothing. There was something in his stance that made me feel like he was ready to leap and rage at any given second. He was less muscular than the other two, with lean, shredded limbs. Less strong but thrice as quick, I assumed. Each man wore head-to-toe camo, a gun on their hip, and a knife secured to their thigh.

Roman jerked his chin to the blaze behind them, redirecting their attention.

Mack shrugged. "Your boy put up quite a fight." He grinned. "He's definitely your brother."

Roman's eyes narrowed on the flames.

Mack continued. "We blocked the road to intercept victim transport, as you instructed. Your boy came barreling around the corner like fucking Mario Andretti. We blew his tires, but the guy hit the gas and drove headfirst into a tree."

Intentional, my guess, knowing he was at the end of his rope."

"He in there?"

Mack shook his head. "Nope. Got him on the way out."

"Did you kill him?"

I noticed a change in Roman's tone, a hint of panic at the thought that his brother might be dead.

"No, man," Mack said. "I get the feeling enough blood has been shed on this mission. He's cuffed, in the back of my truck. Needs medical attention." Mack spat, then checked his nails.

Roman's focus shifted to the Chevy parked haphazardly in the ditch.

"Figured you'd want to do the honors," Mack said.

Ryder tossed Roman the keys to the truck that held his brother.

Roman caught the keys in midair. Turning them over in his palm, he stared down at them. Then he tossed them back.

Frowning, Mack caught the keys. "You don't want to see him? Talk to him, at least? Wrap his balls around his—"

"No." Roman looked at me, then back at the men. "No. Take him to the local PD." He pulled a business card from his wallet. Before he flicked it to Ryder, I caught the name Kieran Healy, CIA written across it.

"Call the man on that card," he said. "Tell him I got him the head of the Cussane Network." Then he reached into his other pocket and tossed Ryder a small silver USB.

"The USB?" My eyes rounded. I'd totally forgotten about it. "You got it?"

Roman smirked. "Why do you think I was allowing my ass to get kicked so badly? Son of a bitch had it secured on a chain to his belt."

I laughed, and Roman winked.

Phineas nodded at the card Ryder was holding. "I know Kieran personally. I'll make sure he gets the message."

"Thanks." Roman refocused on Ryder. "The contents of that USB are everything the CIA needs to blow up a global human-trafficking network. The man on that card will handle it all." Roman wiped his hands, then lifted his palms. "I'm done with it."

Mack glanced at me, a suspicious confusion written over his face. Ryder, on the other hand, hadn't taken his eyes off me, assessing me like one might a poisonous snake.

Roman shifted toward me, protective. "This is—"

"Samantha Greene," Ryder said.

Roman nodded, taking my hand in his. "Sam, this is Mack McCoy and Ryder Jagger, my brothers from Astor Stone. They're agents, like me. And Phineas Decker, apparently, though I can't vouch for him yet."

I caught a playful tone in Roman's voice and got the vibe that there was some hazing yet to do.

"Nice to meet you all," I said.

The men dipped their chins. Ryder grinned at Roman.

Mack shared a similar ornery smirk. "Guess I don't need to know where you got that *S* carved into your wrist."

"I didn't do it," I said quickly, glancing at the line of red scabs coloring Roman's wrist.

"No, I don't think you did," Mack said with a wink.

"All right, as much as I'd love to stand here and catch up," Roman said mockingly, "we've got work to do."

"What's next?"

All three men stepped forward, each pulling his gun from his belt. Ready. I could tell they lived for this kind of life, literally.

"Keep the road blocked," Roman said. "Sam and I will

take the kids to the hospital, then come back and load up the other victims."

"Ah." Ryder nodded to the two little faces pressed against the window of the truck. "I was wondering how long you two had known each other."

"Funny," Roman deadpanned.

"That's Maisie and Marcus," I said. "They were kidnapped in Puerto Vallarta a week ago."

"How many tangos at the house?" Mack asked, checking the cartridge in his gun.

"Four," I said.

Roman smirked proudly. "Sam here bulldozed three of 'em."

The men stared at me, their eyebrows arching.

Mack nodded at me. "Nice work."

"The others?" Ryder asked.

"I took care of them. But more on their way, no doubt. Keep your heads up."

"Aw, man, come on." Mack groaned. "I thought you had a challenge for us. I didn't come all this way for nothing."

"If we come across any more guards, you want them dead or alive?" Ryder asked, interrupting the whining.

"Alive. Round them up, hold them at gunpoint until we get the victims out of the house. Then we'll tie 'em up."

Mack pulled a bag from the bed of his truck and tossed it to Roman. "Suit up."

Roman secured a bulletproof vest on me, then himself. Grinning, he examined me. I grinned back, imagining what I looked like. Dirty hair, dirty face, a yellow sundress under a bulletproof vest.

Then he turned to the men. "Let's do this." He gestured to the truck. "You've got him contained?"

"Oh yeah. If he escapes, he'd have to take the cab of the truck with him."

"Roll out."

Mack paused, glancing back at the flames. "You sure you don't want a piece of him real quick? Don't even want to look into the bloody face of the motherfucker? You sure?"

Roman considered me. "Yeah. Yeah, I'm sure."

The sound of an engine rumbled in the distance, and Phineas cocked his pistol.

Roman glanced at Mack. "More men coming to the lodge. Ambush them."

"You got it, bro." Mack split off, and Phineas and Ryder disappeared into the jungle just as quickly.

Roman grabbed my hand, and together, we jogged to the truck.

56

Two weeks later

The weeks following the incident were a blur of travel, physical healing, and emotional decompressing.

Minutes after we'd rescued the victims from the lodge, the jungle turned into a circus of fire trucks, police cars, and ambulances, every citizen in the nearby small town responding to what they thought was a forest fire.

They got a hell of a lot more than anticipated.

The authorities found Conor Cussane tied to the chassis of a truck, four guards tied to trees, and twelve victims of human trafficking.

Mack, Ryder, and Phineas were ghosts in the wind.

Roman's contact, Kieran, was on the phone with the local authorities within the hour, taking credit for the incident and demanding their cooperation. That night, the CIA agent arrived with a team of federal agents and took over the case.

Roman and I were released from questioning, and somehow, I knew our names would be scrubbed from the file.

After being released from the scene, we'd spent the afternoon hiking to the location of Roman's friend's body. Together, we gave Bear a proper burial, leaving a cross woven of plumeria flowers on his grave.

The next day, we visited the hospital where Maisie and Marcus were being kept for observation. I'll never forget the look on their mother's face as she sat between them, one arm tightly wrapped around Maisie, the other around her son. Once Roman and I confirmed they were of good health, we slipped back into the shadows with smiles on our faces.

The next morning, we were on the first flight out to the States.

By lunchtime, I was back in Oklahoma, in my weeping mother's arms.

By dinnertime, I was back in Roman's arms, in my bed, in my sheets, with Richard at our feet.

Roman never left my side during that time, helping my mother take care of me, helping her with the house, the cooking, the cleaning. Over the weeks, he and my mother formed a bond that made my heart swell.

It was fourteen days of family, healing, and love . . . until Roman nervously requested a trip back to Tenedores, for reasons he didn't offer but seemed emotional about.

I agreed without hesitation, and we—Roman, me, *and* Richard—were on a private flight the next day.

57

SAM

Sunlight twinkled off the white church steeple, a bright beam spotlighting us as we walked across the street.

It was a beautiful day in Mexico, a big bright yellow sun shining in a sapphire-blue sky. The humidity seemed less stifling, and everything was more colorful, more vibrant than I remembered from my last stint in the jungle.

I'd chosen a white sundress and comfortable sandals for the day, unsure what Roman had planned. Apparently, we were going to church.

Roman was wearing his usual T-shirt and khaki tactical pants, except that day, he'd opted for flip-flops instead of boots.

I loved his feet.

"So, this is Tenedores, huh?" I asked. "Where Bear was supposed to meet us and take me to the airport, and you were going to go back and murder Conor Cussane?"

"Yep." He laughed. "'Bout sums it up."

Richard bounded onto the stone steps, his tail wagging

wildly as he sniffed the faded footprints from morning prayer.

"Richard, come." Roman snapped his fingers.

The dog jumped off the steps and obediently trotted to Roman's feet. It appeared the dominating effect Roman had extended beyond just humans.

We pushed through the church door.

The chapel was vacant and silent. Light poured in from the stained glass windows, pooling onto the small altar. Above it was a large cross, glittering in the light.

Roman inhaled deeply as he surveyed the chapel, as if soaking in every inch of it. His expression caught me by surprise. There was a softness in his expression I'd never seen before.

Hand in hand, we walked down the center aisle, Richard close on our heels.

"It's beautiful," I whispered.

Roman nodded, then turned toward the first pew.

He gently released my hand, and for some reason, I knew that the next few minutes were to be his, and his alone. I watched as Roman slowly walked to the center of the pew, eyeing a particular spot.

He pulled a set of keys from his pocket and laid them on the seat.

Covering the key chain with his hand, he bowed his head and whispered, "Thanks, Mom."

A smile crossed his face. Then he opened his eyes and turned toward me.

Butterflies burst to life in my stomach as he closed the space between us, his steps full of intent, his eyes like lasers on mine.

"Marry me," he said in midstride, as if he couldn't wait another second. "Marry me, Samantha." Then he dropped to his knees at my feet, gazing up at me, his eyes filled with so much love, it took my breath away.

Tears filled my eyes, the sudden rush of emotions wiping out my ability to speak.

"Marry me, Samantha Greene. I don't have a ring right now, and I'm sorry for that, but I have never been more sure of anything—not a single thing in my life—than this moment right now. Marry me." He grabbed my hand as tears rolled down my cheeks. "Marry me and make me the happiest man in the world."

"Yes," I whispered, falling to my knees in front of him. "*Yes.*"

He pulled me to him, wrapping me in his arms.

We cried together, rocking back and forth on our knees, right there on the church floor. Letting everything go, releasing the past. Releasing our pain, our guilt, the armor that had slowly formed around us as a result of trauma and pain. The armor that had stolen the light from our souls, confining the darkness and smothering who we once were.

Roman and I started over that day.

Together, we took the first step in finding our way back to the people we used to be, for better or worse.

ABOUT THE AUTHOR

Amanda McKinney is the bestselling and multi-award-winning author of more than twenty romantic suspense and mystery novels. Her book, Rattlesnake Road, was named one of *POPSUGAR's 12 Best Romance Books,* and was featured on the *Today Show.* The fifth book in her Steele Shadows series was recently nominated for the prestigious *Daphne du Maurier Award for Excellence in Mystery/Suspense.* Amanda's books have received over fifteen literary awards and nominations.

Text **AMANDABOOKS** to **66866** to sign up for Amanda's

Newsletter and get the latest on new releases, promos, and freebies!

www.amandamckinneyauthor.com

If you enjoyed HER MERCENARY, please write a review!

Made in the USA
Middletown, DE
14 December 2023